HOMEFREE

NINA WRIGHT

HOMEFREE

Woodbury, Minnesota

First Edition
First Printing, 2006

Book design by Steffani Chambers
Cover design by Lisa Novak
Cover image © 2006 Image Stock
Editing by Rhiannon Ross

Flux, an imprint of Llewellyn Publications

Library of Congress Cataloging-in-Publication Data

Wright, Nina, 1964-
Homefree / Nina Wright.
p. cm.
Summary: Caught in an extremely difficult situation at home and in her new high school, sixteen-year-old Easter's life improves greatly when she is recruited by a mysterious school where teens—all outsiders like herself—develop their paranormal abilities.
ISBN-13: 978-0-7387-0927-7
ISBN-10: 0-7387-0927-1
[1. Family problems--Fiction. 2. High schools--Fiction. 3. Parapsychology--Fiction. 4. Supernatural--Fiction. 5. Schools--Fiction.] I. Title.
PZ7.W95775Hom 2006 [Fic]--dc22 2005058932

Flux
Llewellyn Publications
A Division of Llewellyn Worldwide, Ltd.
2143 Wooddale Drive, Dept. 0-7387-0927-1
Woodbury, MN 55125-2989, U.S.A.
www.llewellyn.com

Printed in the United States of America

Dedication

For my Tampa Bay Writers Group, who joined me early in the journey:

Teddie Aggeles, M. K. Buhler, Rebecca Gall, and Greg Neri.

Acknowledgments

Thanks to the following loyal first readers for their questions and encouragement: Kate Argow, Pamela Asire, Bonnie Brandburg, Richard Pahl, and Nancy Potter.

Gratitude, also, to Barbara Moore for paving the way . . . and Megan Atwood and Andrew Karre for bringing this story home(free).

chapter one
GONE

"*Future perfect,* please. Hello? Are you with us, Mademoiselle?"

Madame Papinchak frowned at me from the front of the room, her heavy black glasses making her look extremely serious. All around me students were whispering.

Good question, I thought, and cleared my throat. "*Je serai venu, tu seras venu, il serai venu—*"

"Cette fille, elle est trop bizarre-oh," boomed a voice behind me. Translation from the Bad French: "That chick is too weird." The class erupted in laughter. Lame jokes in a second language get results.

Mme Papinchak rapped a small wooden mallet against her desk. She used a gavel to keep order in the classroom. A pearl-handled gavel. I figured once upon a time she must have wanted to be a judge or at least a lawyer. Somebody important. Yet she'd ended up here, teaching high school French. What went wrong? Another example of an adult who didn't turn out.

"Order!" Mme Papinchak said, rapping her gavel. *"Attention, s'il vous plaît!"*

When the room quieted, she asked me to start conjugating all over again. This time nobody interrupted. But when the class ended, and students were exiting, I could hear them talking about me. I hadn't made many friends in the two weeks since I'd transferred to Fowler. Okay, I hadn't made a single one. I wasn't sure I wanted to. This school was full of kids I'd never hang out with.

"Could I speak to you a moment?" Mme Papinchak motioned for me to approach her desk. When the room had cleared, she said, "Easter, are you all right?"

"Fine. Why?"

She cocked her head. "For a few minutes there, you seemed very far away."

If you only knew, I thought. But I just waited.

"What I mean is—" Madame hesitated. "Well, you seemed . . . *gone*. Are you sure you're all right?"

That was code for "Are you sober?" Which ticked me off. I didn't get high.

Mme Papinchak tugged on a strand of her straight, shoulder-length hair like she was trying to pull out the right words.

"I know it's stressful to move to a new school when the term's almost over," she said finally. "Perhaps you'd like to talk to a counselor?"

I had to strain not to roll my eyes. "I'm fine."

"I'm not prying, Easter." Of course she was. "But it was like you were—I don't know—off the map. To be honest, you scared me."

I had scared myself. Madame was right. While conjugating, I went off the map, and I couldn't begin to explain what had happened. Right in the middle of fourth-period French class, I was suddenly standing in the downstairs half-bathroom of the house where I used to live when I was twelve.

I was sixteen now and living in Tampa, Florida. Yet that was my face, my *current* face with the new emerald nose stud, gazing back at me in the mirror at 47 Monarch Street. In Muncie, Indiana. I lived there four unhappy moves and more than a thousand miles ago . . . How could I be in Indiana when I was also somewhere else?

I studied the half-bathroom as it came into focus. The new owners hadn't bothered to replace the crimson-foil wallpaper Mom hated. I used to secretly like the tacky, almost Christmassy way it brightened the windowless room. Now it just looked shabby, as if the kids who came along after me had taken turns peeling the paper from what used to be an invisible seam.

What is this? I wondered. A dream? A hallucination? A memory twisted by wishful thinking? I blinked twice but remained standing on the stained, gray linoleum of my family's former bathroom.

My eyes wandered to the wood molding around the bathroom door, where Dad used to measure me on birthdays. Nobody had bothered to repaint. The dark pencil marks were still there although it looked like somebody had tried to erase them. I stepped closer. The highest one barely came to my shoulder. Next to a thick dash were the blurred words "EASTER HUTTON, age 11."

Tears burned my eyes. This was the only home where I had ever been happy—a house I hadn't been near since I was twelve.

I studied my trembling hands. All jewelry accounted for, including my favorite and newest treasure: the pewter armor ring Andrew gave me as a parting gift when I left Atlanta.

Footsteps in the hall shot a ripple of panic through me. I leaped back against the sink. How could I explain to a stranger what I couldn't begin to explain to myself?

"Hi. You don't know me, but I used to live here. Don't worry, I don't have a weapon. Or a clue how I got here from Florida. Last thing I knew I was conjugating the verb *venir . . .*"

The door, already ajar, swung toward me. I tensed for a screech of fright. Women scream. Men yelp—or start throwing punches. I looked around for a way to defend myself. The plunger we used to keep by the toilet might have worked, but it was gone.

Somewhere in the house a phone rang. The door froze in mid-swing. A voice on the other side cried, "If that's for me, I'm already gone!"

It was a throaty voice, more like a loud purr than a shout. The door opened the rest of the way, and in stepped a big blonde, maybe a year older than me. The bathroom was tiny. I had no room to move.

"I won't hurt you!" I declared before she could react.

But she didn't react. She didn't seem to notice me. She just peered into the mirror, tilting her head from side to side, fluffing her tousled hair. I stared as our reflections overlapped. The blonde was standing where I was standing. We were in the same place at the same time. Or were we? Our faces blurred and separated and blurred again.

To steady myself I grabbed the towel bar, which felt rubbery and unstable. I was really there, in that bathroom. But the blonde couldn't see me.

"Amber called!" a man's voice thundered. "She said she'll do what you told her to do."

The blonde stopped primping. She studied her reflection—what I saw as our combined reflections—with satisfaction, her lips pulling up at the corners in what would have been a smile if her eyes had played along. They stayed dark and hard. In her furry little voice, she muttered, "She'd better. Amber better do exactly what I say."

To the man somewhere in the house where I used to live, the blonde shouted, "I'm leaving!"

Then she was gone, and so was I—back to Fowler High and my totally screwed-up life.

Now I faced Mme Papinchak, who looked as worried as I was trying not to feel.

"I'm fine," I repeated and walked away.

You can find Muncie, Indiana, on a map, but not the route I'd taken.

The second time I went "off the map" was during third-period geometry two days later. Mr. Rivera was droning on about something called a conic section when I found myself in the attic bedroom I used to share with my stepsister in Wheeling, West Virginia. And I wasn't alone.

The first occupant who came into focus had four legs. It was Rocco the tuxedo cat, who looked even fatter and scruffier than the last time I'd seen him, two years ago. I called Rocco "Serial Killer Cat." He had tortured about a thousand mice, birds, rabbits, and baby squirrels to death. And he always left their mangled corpses by the back door. Mom said they were supposed to be gifts for us, but they made me sick. Plus, Rocco had a habit of hiding under the decaying cars my stepfather collected around the yard. The cat would shoot out from under them and attack my ankles whenever I walked past. I had scabs on my legs the whole year I lived there.

Now Rocco looked smug and sassy, sprawled on the bed I used to sleep in. Was that the same comforter Mom bought me at Wal-Mart for my thirteenth birthday? It was so covered with cat hair I couldn't be sure. I leaned forward for a closer look, and suddenly Rocco turned to face me, his yellow eyes open wide. His tail snapped back and forth, and his back arched.

Yeeeooooowwwww, he screeched.

He could see me. I stumbled backwards against what felt from memory like the bi-fold closet door. Rocco yowled again.

"Shut up, you stupid cat!"

That was when I spotted the room's other occupant: my former stepsister Ronni (short for Veronica), lounging on the bed at the far end of the room. What time was it here? Shouldn't she be at school?

Rocco produced another threatening sound. He stared at me, ears flattened, lips curled back. All the hair on his round body stood on end. I held my breath, wondering how things worked in this version of the world. Could Rocco hurt me? And if he could see me, could Ronni see me, too?

Something large and hard thudded against the wall an inch from my right ear, then ricocheted into Rocco. The cat screamed, launched himself straight up off the floor, and was gone.

"Go kill something, why don't you?" Ronni shouted after him.

You almost did, I thought, my heart banging. I studied my ex-step-sib. Still skinny like when we were both thirteen, but now she had boobs so round they looked like implants. Clear skin, too. Wearing a sports bra and matching boxers, Ronni sat propped against a stack of pillows nodding to the rhythms of an MP3 player and painting her toenails purple. Her formerly shoulder-length, ash-blonde hair was now spiked into inch-long tufts. She was still too cute to tolerate.

I checked the floor. Ronni had lobbed a running shoe, a *huge* running shoe, at the cat. No way it could belong to her dad, who was practically a midget. I winced at the memory of Short Ron with his pudgy arm around Mom's thin waist. Short Ron wasn't my nickname for him. It was the nickname he'd created for himself and his doomed used-car dealership. The marriage had been short, too. And doomed.

From downstairs, a guy bellowed something. Definitely not Short Ron, who had a squeaky voice. This voice was deep but muffled, like whoever was shouting had a mouthful of food. When Ronni didn't answer, the other person came pounding up the stairs.

I wasn't prepared for the guy with no shoes, no shirt, and what looked like a six-layer bologna sandwich who appeared in Ronni's doorway. It was my middle-school boyfriend, Cal. Only he wasn't scrawny anymore. At sixteen, he looked all grown up and totally buff. Cal launched himself onto Ronni's bed and tried to kiss her.

"Gross!" she shrieked. "I'm doing my nails, moron! Get away from me!"

Ronni's shrill voice could pierce your eardrums. Cal laughed, rolled off the bed onto the floor, and took another bite of his sandwich. Maybe he was a moron. When he turned his smooth, naked back toward me, I read the Gothic-lettered tattoo across his shoulder blades: WACKER. That was his last name, but not the smartest choice in tattoos. I recalled Mom's warning: "Cal's sweet, hon, but he'll always be one bottle short of a six-pack." Mom knew the ways men could let you down.

Even so, I was enjoying my private view of Cal's new muscles when I felt Mr. Rivera tapping my textbook with his pointer.

"I said, write the proof for problem six on the board. Now!" he barked.

Cal's tattoo shimmered and faded. I was back in geometry class. Mr. Rivera leaned close to my ear.

"If you can hear what I'm saying, blink twice." He was trying to be funny, and it worked. My classmates yucked it up.

"You must be talented, Easter. You can sleep with your eyes wide open," Mr. Rivera said. "But that won't save your math grade."

"Or your social life," quipped the guy next to me, and the class roared again.

It was the same jock who'd told the lame French joke two days earlier. No more insults for free.

"How's your ex in St. Augustine?" I demanded. "The one you got pregnant last year? Do you even call her?"

I had no clue where the words were coming from. It was like someone had turned on a radio, only it was my mouth. And I couldn't turn it off or change the station.

"Do you support your son? Have you ever even seen him?"

Except for my voice, the room was totally quiet. I could hear people breathing.

"He's six months old, you know, old enough to have a personality. Old enough to recognize the people he loves. And he has your eyes."

The classroom swallowed a collective gasp, and the preppy girl in front of me whispered, "Dustin, you make me sick. You said Kayla *lied* about the baby being yours."

"She did!" the jock sputtered, but his face was scarlet. To me he said, "You're seriously messed up. You should keep your mouth shut."

Mr. Rivera rapped his pointer three times on Dustin's desk. Mme Papinchak's gavel would have been more effective.

"That's enough!" he bellowed. "More than enough! Back to geometry: problem six. Who has the answer? Katie, go to the board. You, too, Darnell. Write your proofs!"

And so I was spared the embarrassment of not knowing how to solve problem six. If only I could have escaped my real problems that easily.

chapter two
ALONE

I remember my seventh-grade language arts teacher saying, "Libraries are sanctuaries." She probably meant they're the perfect place to hang out with books and your imagination. But I chose Fowler High's library to be my sanctuary for another reason: I was in big trouble with about half the student body, and I needed a place to hide.

It was three hours since the incident in geometry class. Word was traveling fast that Easter Hutton was "crazy" or "evil" or both. Skipping school for a couple weeks looked like a good idea. Leaving forever looked better.

I might as well have foamed at the mouth or announced that I had a hideous contagious disease. Broadcasting the personal secrets of Dustin Yarvich, star jock, was the sure death of my social life before I'd even decided if I wanted one. I'd be odd girl out for the rest of my days. So, while everybody else headed for their cars or the bus line, I made a beeline to the library.

For a while I sat in a study cubicle and stared at the school librarian. Talk about a loser job. Who wants to go to college and grad school just to keep kids from mis-shelving books or talking too loud? And that got me thinking. What is a good job? One that pays really well and doesn't require sucking up. Being president, maybe, but first you have to get elected, and that means sucking up to the whole country. Running your own company could be good, but first you'd have to invent a product or service that everybody wanted. That sounded like sucking up, too.

I had no interest in pleasing people. In fact, I was perfecting the art of not caring what anybody thought about me. For years I had watched Mom try to please man after man only to get cheated on or dumped. "Playing to Please" was a game you couldn't win. "Playing to Please Yourself" might be all right. Trouble was, I hadn't figured out how to please myself. Everything I really wanted was something I didn't have the power to keep in my life, like my dad and my best friend, Andrew.

I waited until the last student had left the computer cubicles. Then I slid into the farthest booth. If I couldn't be around Andrew anymore, at least we could exchange email. Sometimes instant messaging seemed like the only thing keeping me sane. Although I didn't have a PC at home, I used the ones at school.

My message center announced that Andrew was online. Quickly I typed:

> HELP! I'M A PRISONER IN A FASCIST FLORIDA HIGH SCHOOL! I FEEL LIKE I'M LOSING MY MIND.

Andrew replied with a crazy-faced emoticon and

> YOU WERE DOOMED AT BIRTH. INSANITY IS GENETIC . . . HOW'S LIFE WITH WACKY MAMA?
>
> Me: AT LEAST SHE STOPPED PUKING. NOW SHE JUST CRIES ALL THE TIME . . .
>
> Andrew: ANY NEWS FROM HER MAYBE NEXT HUSBAND?
>
> Me: HE STOPPED CALLING. I THINK WE'RE SCREWED AGAIN. AND THIS TIME MOM LANDED US IN HOT-WEATHER HELL. WE'RE NOT EVEN IN THE PART OF FLORIDA WHERE WE USED TO LIVE, WHERE I ACTUALLY KNEW A FEW KIDS. I HATE HATE HATE IT HERE!!!!

Andrew: SORRY, BABY. REALLY SORRY. ARE YOU WEARING THE RING? IF YOU BELIEVE IN THE POWER OF OUR FRIENDSHIP, IT WILL PROTECT YOU.

Me: RIGHT. LIKE SANTA, THE EASTER BUNNY, AND A BAND OF LEPRECHAUNS.

Andrew: NO, THIS WORKS BECAUSE WEARING IT REMINDS YOU THAT WE'RE ONE IN SPIRIT AND CONNECTED *ALL THE TIME.* I CARE ABOUT HOW YOU'RE DOING EVERY DAY.

My vision blurred. I wiped my eyes with the back of one hand and blinked at the pewter armor ring on the other.

Me: HOW'S IT GOING WITH MARCO?

Andrew: SLOW. SOMETIMES I THINK I KNOW MORE ABOUT HIM THAN HE'S READY TO TELL ME.

Me: MAYBE HE'S NOT READY TO COME OUT. MAYBE HIS PARENTS AREN'T AS COOL AS YOURS.

Andrew: MY PARENTS AREN'T COOL, THEY ARE IN DENIAL. THEY THINK BEING GAY IS A PHASE. THEY'LL STILL BE THINKING THAT WHEN I'M 50.

Me: THEY'LL BE DEAD WHEN YOU'RE 50.

Andrew's parents were like twenty years older than everybody else's. Most people thought they were his grandparents. He typed:

I HOPE NOT. I'D LIKE THEM TO LIVE A LONG TIME. SOMEDAY THEY'LL GET USED TO ME BEING THE WAY I AM.

Me: LIKE I GOT USED TO MY MOM BEING THE WAY SHE IS?

Andrew: YOUR MOM'S CRAZY. CAN'T MAKE GOOD DECISIONS FOR LOVE OR MONEY.

Me: KEEPS GOING AFTER BOTH. NEVER ENDS UP WITH EITHER. PROBLEM IS I'M ALONG FOR EVERY RIDE. THIS ONE TOTALLY SUCKS.

Andrew: AT LEAST YOU GOT BEACHES DOWN THERE, RIGHT?

Me: IN THE NEXT COUNTY. DO I HAVE A CAR???

Andrew: DOESN'T THE TRAILER PARK HAVE A POOL?

Me: WE'RE SUPPOSED TO CALL IT A VILLAGE. YEAH, THERE'S A POOL IF YOU DON'T MIND HANGING OUT WITH CREEPS AND UGLIES. EVERYBODY WHO LIVES THERE IS ANCIENT. THE OLD LADIES WANT TO KNOW ABOUT MY FAMILY. THE OLD MEN STARE AT ME WITH THEIR MOUTHS OPEN AND THEY DON'T HAVE ALL THEIR TEETH.

Andrew: I WISH YOU COULD COME BACK TO ATLANTA.

I teared up again, which pissed me off because I hate to cry and almost never do it. Atlanta hadn't been good, either, except for Andrew, who was as much of an outsider as I was.

Now I was far away from everybody I'd ever loved. This place felt like the lonesome end of a long, bumpy road.

Since I had deliberately missed the last school bus, I took my time walking home to Amber Sands Estates. The late afternoon sun was blazing, and my route offered no shade trees (you can't count palms). It wasn't like Mom and I lived in some quiet suburb, either. Amber Sands was at the intersection of two major Tampa highways. After an hour plodding along glaring concrete sidewalks, inhaling exhaust fumes, and listening to car horns and catcalls, I was soaked with sweat. And depressed.

"Home" was a sagging single-wide trailer. Once it had probably been white. Now it was stained and dingy with broken awnings, a missing step, a rasping air conditioner in one window, and yellow shades in all the others. I paused outside the only door. Sometimes I could hear Mom crying before I even went inside. Not today. The air conditioner coughed and moaned in a chorus with neighboring units, making the only sound there was.

The metal door yelped when I yanked it open. I listened again. Still no sobbing sounds. Either Mom was asleep or away. Our car had been in the shop since the day we rolled into Florida, so it was hard to tell when she was out.

"Hellooo! Easter, honey!" The warble came from over my right shoulder. Trudy the Nosy Neighbor waddled toward me waving both hands.

"Your mom's not home, honey!" she wheezed. "Glad I caught you! No point sitting in there all alone, especially when your air conditioner don't hardly work. Nikki—I mean, your mom—told me you two just can't get cool over there."

Since when is that your concern, I wondered. Though panting, Trudy forced a grandmotherly smile. "You come on over to my house and we'll have us some nice cold tea."

"Where's my mom?" If I could hear anxiety in my voice, I was pretty sure Trudy could, too.

"Everything's going to be fine," she said, way too cheerfully. "You come refresh yourself in my nice cool kitchen, and we can talk. No need for us to stand here melting—"

She touched my arm, and I jerked away. "I said, where's my mom?"

Trudy's face morphed from fake-friendly to annoyed. She took a step back and said, "No need to tell the whole village, either. Let's keep this between you and me. Are you coming or not?" She started toward her own trailer, a sunshine-yellow single-wide less than ten feet away. Behind her back, Mom and I called it the Tin Daisy.

"Like everybody doesn't already know we got problems," I called after her.

Trudy turned to face me, hands on hips. "You might be surprised. Truth is, most folks don't care about other people's business. Now, if you want to know what's happening with your mom, you'll come on over. I told her I'd take care of you."

I wanted to tell Nosy Trudy that I didn't need taking care of. All I needed was to know where my mom was. This wasn't the first time a neighbor had shown up to explain her absence. It was just the first time in Tampa.

Trudy wouldn't tell me anything until we had our cold tea in front of us. She made me wait on her plastic yellow sofa with the AC blasting the back of my neck while she bumped around a kitchen the size of a phone booth.

Finally, she lowered herself onto the cushion next to me and took a long sip from her jelly-jar glass. When she put her drink down, she was wearing that grandmotherly expression again.

"Easter, honey, it's about the baby."

My breath scraped against my ribs. "Is Mom all right? What happened?" Then it hit me. "How do *you* know about the baby?"

"Nikki got sick in the laundry room the day after you got here. I knew right away she was pregnant."

"Is she all right?" I repeated.

Trudy drew a breath. "Honey—I think your mom had a miscarriage. She couldn't stop bleeding and got real scared. Came pounding on my door, her face white as a sheet. Said she got blood all over everything."

"Blood?" My stomach did a somersault.

"Don't worry. I went and cleaned up best I could after the ambulance left. But there's bloody towels in the laundry basket. I didn't want you to see them and get scared."

I tried to erase the nightmarish pictures by squeezing my eyes shut. Trudy thought I was fighting back tears. She patted my hand.

"Now, now, your mom'll be all right. But I'm afraid you're not getting a new little brother or sister. Not this time."

If Trudy only knew. I didn't want that baby any more than my mom did, but it was the reason we were in Florida. That baby was my mom's best hope. And mine, too.

chapter three
HOPELESS

I explained to Trudy that my mom was in the habit of taking back her maiden name after each divorce. That's why her last name didn't match mine. Trudy agreed that no woman wants to keep using the name of a man who has done her wrong. We discussed all this while Trudy was on hold. She had called the hospital and asked at least six different people what was happening with Nikki Sarno. So far nobody knew.

"I'm sure she'll call us just as soon as she can," Trudy said, her fake smile back in place. "I bet they stuck her in one of those examining rooms, and she can't get to a phone."

Trudy said hospitals have to do a lot of paperwork on every patient, so we should wait for them to finish before we called again. To kill time, we watched two sitcoms with ridiculously happy endings.

The next time Trudy called the hospital, she still couldn't find out anything about my mom. Behind her smile, I could see she was getting anxious, too.

"Maybe I'll just go over there," I said, standing up for a stretch. Trudy's crowded trailer was closing in on me. "Where's the hospital?"

That made Trudy drop her smile. "We'd have to find somebody to drive you."

She didn't own a car and couldn't drive anyway because she had a "condition." Like Mom, she either bummed rides with neighbors or took the bus. Our '93 Ford Taurus was ready at Bob's Good Garage *if* we had the money to claim it. We'd blown a head gasket at the end of the big move from Atlanta and owed three times as much for repairs as we used to pay in rent.

"I can walk," I told Trudy. "Just give me directions."

"It's too far, and it's getting dark. Let me call Joe Jennati. He's always glad to help out."

Joe Jennati had chest hair that reminded me of a white poodle and breath that smelled like dirty socks. "No thanks," I said. "I'll take the bus."

Trudy checked the daisy-shaped wall clock next to her refrigerator.

"Number 44 goes to Our Mother of Mercy, but the next one's in two minutes. You'll have to run." She grabbed a fistful of coins from the ash tray on top of her TV. "Use the tokens for the bus and the change to call me when you get there. I want to hear how she's doing the minute you find out."

Number 44 and I reached the corner at the same time. The bus was half-full of late commuters wilted from the heat or their jobs or both. Panting, I slid into my seat. As we lurched past look-alike gas stations and strip malls, I quickly lost interest in the scenery.

If Trudy was right, and there was no more baby, where would Mom and I go next? I knew one thing for sure: James Dean Bakeman wouldn't care.

Mom used to work as a waitress at the restaurant he managed in Atlanta. When he got her pregnant, there was another problem—*two* more problems: (1) James Dean Bakeman was married, and (2) his wife's family owned the restaurant.

But James Dean had plenty of ideas. I overheard him and my mom arguing about them night after night. First, he asked her to have an abortion. She said she couldn't do that because of her religion. What a crock. Mom never went to church. Or even prayed, as far as I knew.

Next, James Dean suggested she give the baby up for adoption.

"This could be God's way of telling you to be grateful for the kid you got. This could be a sign that you're supposed to give the baby to somebody who really wants one."

"I really want one! I want *your* baby!" my mom wailed.

James Dean's next idea was slow in coming. He said he'd need some time to sort matters out, so we didn't see him for a couple weeks. I worried that my mom would start drinking again, but she didn't. She'd sworn off alcohol for the baby. When James Dean returned, he told Mom that he would marry her and be a father to the baby. Never mind that he was already married with two little kids at home. He said he would get a divorce. He said he would figure it out, but it might take time.

"Divorce is tricky for men," he explained. "They can lose everything if they're not careful. You don't want me to lose everything, do you?"

This was James Dean's best idea: He would get my mom and me out of Atlanta before his wife and her family found out. The plan was to set us up in Tampa, where he was sure he could get work managing a restaurant just as soon as his divorce was done. Until then, Mom and I could stay for free in a mobile home that belonged to James Dean's uncle. The uncle spent half the year in Florida, the other half up north somewhere. His trailer sat empty from April through October.

Mom seemed happy, which made me nervous because I knew it couldn't last. James Dean Bakeman helped us pack up our apartment and plan our route to Amber Sands Estates. He even gassed up our car, filled our tires, and gave Mom $500 in cash to get us started. As he waved goodbye, I made the mistake of asking Mom why she thought this guy was better than the other losers she'd hooked up with. She didn't reply until we had rounded the corner out of sight of James Dean. Then she pulled over to the curb and smacked me so hard that my left ear rang for an hour.

Reality check: If James Dean Bakeman found out he didn't absolutely have to get a divorce, why would he? He might have already decided it wasn't necessary now that we were gone. Truth was, he hadn't sent us a penny since we got here even though he knew we had no car, no phone, and nobody in Tampa.

That was the dark corner where my thoughts hovered when the bus belched to a stop in front of Our Mother of Mercy Hospital. The soulless square building was painted flat white. Even the sun's slanting rays couldn't dance on it. I tried to remember the last time I'd been inside a hospital and then, remembering, wished I hadn't. All hospitals have the same stink of bleach and fear.

I found my way to the information desk and asked what room Nikki Sarno was in. A blue-haired woman who seemed to have trouble lining her eyes up with her glasses made a face at the computer screen.

"Hmm—a new admit on the fifth floor. Are you immediate family?"

"I am her only family. I'm her daughter. What room is she in?"

The woman pulled her head back like a turtle ducking into its shell. "You're not familiar with the fifth floor?"

Of course I wasn't.

She dropped her voice so low that I had to lean in to catch the words. "That's the psychiatric unit. You'll have to check in at the desk up there and see if they'll let you visit. Good luck."

Too late for that. Numbly I located the nearest guest elevator and rode up alone, noticing that universal hospital smell creeps into elevators, too. I wished the ride took longer since I had no clue what to say if they did let me see my mom. She must have freaked out when they told her the baby was dead. Why else would she be in the wacko unit instead of wherever they put you if you'd just lost a lot of blood?

I wondered if I should let on that I already knew the baby was gone. Should I act sad? Or would that push Mom over the edge? If I pretended like it was all for the best, she might fly into a rage and yell that I'd never wanted the baby. On the other hand, if I acted like I didn't know what was going on, then she'd have to tell me, and that would upset her all over again for sure. My head was starting to hurt. Maybe I'd get lucky and find her too drugged to talk. That way I wouldn't have to say anything till she was well enough to come home. Then I'd have plenty of time to rehearse.

The nurse on duty, whose nametag read R. DEENER, nodded encouragingly when I explained why I was there.

"Your mother was asking about you." R. Deener checked a folder on her desk. "I tried to notify family, but there was no answer at the number in Atlanta."

James Dean Bakeman, armed with Caller ID, had probably stopped taking calls from this area code.

R. Deener was still reading her notes. "How old are you, Easter?"

"Eighteen." You get a lot less crap if people think you're an adult.

"Then you can visit for fifteen minutes. Just let me tell your mother you're here."

Too nervous to sit, I paced around the fake-cozy waiting room with its overstuffed plaid sofa and matching chairs. The whole point was to distract you from the fact that you were visiting a person who needed to be locked away.

"Easter?" Finally R. Deener was back. "Your mother can see you now. She's waiting in the Sun Room."

That won't put her in a good mood, I thought, knowing how my mom hates natural light. Another reason the whole Florida move was doomed. Mom always whined that she had sun-sensitive skin and eyes. She'd rather spend her days in a dark room—like a bar, for example—than on a beach. It was why she liked the restaurant business: the light was usually low.

R. Deener led me through a double doorway down a rose-colored hall past a TV room. I could feel the eyes of messed-up inmates drilling into me, but I focused on the nurse's blue-smocked back.

She paused outside another set of double doors. "I'll come and get you when your time is up. Then we'll need to talk for a moment."

"About what?"

"I just need to ask a few questions for your mom's file. Ready to go in?"

I swallowed. "How is she? Really?"

"I'm sure she's much better, now that you're here."

"Should I—you know—be careful about . . . what I say?"

R. Deener smiled. "Just be yourself. Your mom will let you know what she wants to talk about. She's on medication, so she may seem a little foggy. Don't worry, that's normal."

Mom was frequently foggy. But "normal" was not a word I had ever used to describe her. R. Deener opened the door to a room that looked too warm to belong in a hospital. The red-gold light of a Florida sunset poured through the wide windows, washing Mom's pale skin and hair a rich coral. The only person in the room, she looked fragile in the big wingback chair. At first she was staring into the air, a sad, empty expression in her eyes. Then she turned to me and reached out a hand. Maybe I hesitated because she said, "Would it kill you to give me a hug?"

I did, pressing my face into her hair like I used to when I was a kid. I wasn't sure which of us needed comfort most. As usual, Mom smelled like an ash tray.

"I've been through hell," she sighed.

I was having a rough day myself, but I decided not to say so. A neutral approach seemed best. "Are you all right?"

Mom made a sniffling noise. "Didn't Trudy tell you what happened? The baby's gone."

"So why are you here?" I hoped I wouldn't have to be more specific. I didn't want to say "in the loony bin."

"Who knows." She shrugged. "I guess I said . . . some things. I got a little crazy."

"What do you mean?"

"Maybe I said something about killing myself. I can't remember." Mom rubbed her forehead. "You know how important that baby was. For our future."

"We'll be all right," I said, although I didn't believe it. What if she couldn't get herself together? What if they really did lock her away?

Mom looked at me, eyes shining. "I didn't plan this, Easter. We were supposed to be happy."

"We'll still be happy," I lied, sliding onto the floor at her feet so that I could take her hands in mine. They were so cold. How could they be so cold with the sun pouring in on them?

Mom yanked her hands away and did what she always did when things turned terrible: she buried her face in them. Yes, she was crying, but I figured she mostly wanted to hide.

"Nothing ever works out for me," she moaned.

How often had I heard that? It was her all-purpose all-time excuse.

"You could change things," I said quietly. "You could try . . ."

Instantly she stopped crying. It was as if I'd flipped a switch, but her hands stayed in place.

"I lost my baby!" she announced, like I'd missed the news flash. "My life sucks!"

"Yeah, well, so does mine, but I'm not crying about it."

Mom's hands came away from her red-rimmed eyes. "You didn't just lose your whole future. That baby meant everything to me."

"Glad to know I'm so important," I snapped.

"Of course you are," she said and reached for me, but I was on my feet. "It's just that you're almost grown up. You have your own life already. What about mine?"

At the edge of my vision, the room was turning red—blood red. My ears roared like the surf.

"You're a selfish, pathetic loser," I heard myself shout. "You know what? I'm glad you lost the baby. Now you won't be a rotten mother to one more kid."

That would have been Mom's cue to smack me. But I didn't give her the chance. I didn't wait for R. Deener to tell me our time was up, either. The room was darkening to wine red, the noise in my head engulfing me like a tidal wave. I stumbled toward the exit, but I couldn't find the door.

Suddenly I felt the floor shift under my feet. I seemed to be sliding from tile onto soft carpet. Then I recognized the smell of boiled cabbage that used to seep through the vents in our furnished Atlanta apartment. I was back where Mom and I had lived until the end of last month.

But a different tenant was there now, and he had already moved the couch. A very old, bald man sat dozing in front of the TV, his head nodding over his chest. Instantly his chin jerked up.

"Who's there?" he called in a cracked voice. "Is that you, Easter? What the devil took you so long?"

chapter four
CRACKED

"Who are you?" I demanded as soon as I could catch my breath. "And why did you move the couch? You can't even see the TV from there."

"I'll ask the questions," the old man croaked.

And then it hit me: this was the first time a person who lived where I had landed could see me. In fact, he knew my name and seemed to be expecting me.

"What am I doing here?" I said. "And how do you know me?"

The old man cocked his head and frowned. I noticed that his eyes were milky blue, almost white.

"What did I say about asking questions?" he growled.

"This is way too weird," I mumbled and started looking around. Everything except the couch seemed pretty much the way Mom and I had left it. Or so I thought until a large green and yellow bird fluttered into the room. I yelped and ducked my head.

The old man cackled. "So you're scared of parrots, are you?"

"You can't have pets in this building," I pointed out, remembering the little girl downstairs telling me that the landlord had made her give up her kitten.

"Do I look like someone who follows the rules?" he barked.

I thought he looked like a crazy person, but I wasn't about to say so. Instead, I stepped closer. "Are you going to tell me who you are, or are you going to make me guess?"

The bird, who had settled on the back of the couch near the old man's right shoulder, flapped its wings and cawed. "Funny girl, she's a funny girl!"

"Not really," I muttered.

"Oh, grow up," snapped the bird.

"Like I'm not trying!" Great. Now I was talking to a parrot. "I want some answers," I told the old man. "I want to know what's happening to me."

"What if I don't have answers? What if I only have questions?" he replied.

"Then what good are you?" I fumed. "I need somebody who can help me!"

"Why don't you ask the right questions?" he said.

"Listen to Mr. Fairless! Listen to Mr. Fairless!" cried the bird.

"Is that your name?" I asked the man.

"Would you rather call me Mr. F?"

I took a deep breath. "Okay, Mr. F, here's the deal: My life is out of control. I mean—*look.*" I pointed at myself and then at the room around me. "I don't even know how I got here. Let alone why. My mom's stuck on the fifth floor, I'm doomed at my new school, and now I'm—I don't know—'astral-projecting' to places where I used to live."

Mr. F didn't move. He didn't even blink. Finally he said, "What's the question?"

My heart thundered.

"What's the question?" I echoed. "What's *not* a question? Where do I start?"

"Pick one, Funny Girl," snapped the parrot.

“Okay, sure,” I said, my eyes stinging with tears of frustration. “My question is . . . *how?* How am I supposed to deal with my life?”

Suddenly, the bird—who seemed too big to be a parrot—launched itself off the couch and flew straight at my face. I jerked away so fast that I tumbled backwards over the footstool, the other piece of furniture the old man must have moved

“Wudja like an answer? Wudja like an answer?” the bird sang out as it circled my head.

“Yes! I want answers!” I lay sobbing on the floor of what used to be my home, fear and anger flowing out of me like water from a shattered vase.

At least the bird didn't crap on me. I decided that was something to be grateful for when I found myself riding the Number 44 through Tampa toward Amber Sands. I had no idea what time it was or how I'd gotten on the bus, but I was sure I was back in reality, whatever that was.

What happened after I asked my “how” question and Wudja went off on me? I remember the bird squawking and Mr. Fairless leaning in close, his breath hot, dry, and garlicky. He didn't ask me if I was all right even though his scruffy bird had practically attacked me, and I had fallen over his stupid footstool. Instead, he whispered something I couldn't quite understand. Something about "special talents." Whatever he said, I must have stopped crying. My cheeks were dry now, and my eyes didn't burn. But here's the weird part (okay, the weird*est*): although I couldn't remember eating anything, I tasted pineapple as sharply as if I'd just swallowed a fresh juicy slice. I should add that ordinarily I hate pineapple, but this tasted good.

Back at Amber Sands, Trudy was still waiting, and she wasn't happy. I'd forgotten to phone her from the hospital. She said she got so worried that she had to take a nerve pill. I felt like telling her to take another one. Instead, I invented a story about why my mom was still in the hospital, something about her losing too much blood. Trudy seemed to buy it.

Alone in our stuffy trailer, I slept pretty well considering my mom was in the psycho ward and I could be heading there myself. What else explained Mr. F and his feathered friend? Not to mention my other recent "trips," plus the way I had broadcasted Dustin Yarvich's secret at dear old Fowler High. While I was sleeping, I must have changed my mind about skipping school. I woke up at the usual time and automatically started getting dressed. When I looked in the mirror, I saw a calmer, more determined version of me. It was like I had to get myself over one big hurdle before anybody had time to build more.

As it turned out, a whole obstacle course was already in place. I was climbing the tile steps to the front entrance of the school when somebody—I never saw who—lobbed a couple eggs against the back of my head. Raw eggs. Then a herd of kids shouted something about "Easter eggs as cracked as Easter Hutton."

Game on.

chapter five
WAVY

I was in the bathroom at Fowler High, washing raw egg off my neck, when I suddenly felt dizzy. So I leaned against the cool tile wall for support and closed my eyes. Very close by, I heard:

"The whole idea is to make her suffer. She's a loser, and she always will be. We're doing her a favor by teaching her that."

The words were chilling enough, but the way the girl said them froze my heart. She spoke with the kind of cold, sick passion you'd expect of serial killers or kids who torture animals. Even worse, her voice was vaguely familiar.

"So when she starts to cry—and sooner or later, in front of everybody, she will cry—we don't let up. Got it?"

There was a murmur of agreement. I was torn between running for my life and sticking around to confront my enemies.

A second female voice: "So, we keep messing with her till . . . when?"

The first voice again: "Till forever. Till she drops out or transfers to a different school."

"What about when school's out?"

"We don't stop messing with her just because it's summer. We know where she lives. Amber Reston will never get it, and she'll never get a break."

Suddenly I figured out where I was: still in a school restroom, yes, but not at Fowler High. I was back in Muncie, Indiana, listening to the blonde from Monarch Street with the furry voice. Far off, I heard lockers being slammed, kids shouting, feet shuffling. I looked down at my own feet. There was egg yolk on my black high-tops. I must have been zapped here directly from Fowler.

But wait. Was it my warped brain, or did my feet look . . . wavy? Like the edges of your vision, just before you get a migraine. I checked out my hands and arms. They were there, they were solid, but they had the same weird shimmer as my feet. I hadn't noticed that during previous projections. Then again, the scenery was so freaky on the first trips that I hadn't thought much about my body. Now I wondered if the shimmer meant that nobody who belonged here could see me.

Suddenly, the stall door swung out instead of in (whose brilliant design was that?), and I took it right on the nose. If we had been in my world, I would have been gushing blood. This didn't hurt much—more like getting pinched than punched. But I staggered back in surprise and grabbed my nose. When I glanced up again, there she was: the big blonde from Muncie. Did she forget to flush?

"Amber thinks she can get us to like her, so we make her do what we want. I don't ever want to hear 'I feel sorry for her.'" The blonde made the last part sound sing-song and added, "Armbruster better not wimp out on us."

"She won't if she knows what's good for her," declared the second voice just before its owner flushed her toilet. A small angular girl emerged from the stall, moving like someone pushing her way through a crowd. "Armbruster doesn't call the shots on this team."

"Right, Jolene," said the blonde.

Just then a tall, athletic-looking girl with frizzy dark blonde curls came in from the hall. She stopped short when she saw the other two. Then she stepped up to the sink and started washing her hands.

"We were just talking about you," Jolene said. "About how you'd better not feel sorry for Amber. We're going to do what we're going to do. And you're going to help us."

"But what if Amber's mom calls the school?" the tall girl asked, studying her soapy hands.

Jolene said, "Amber's mom's in jail, remember?"

The blonde added, "She lives with Grandma now, and Grandma's way too old to save Amber."

The girl jock rinsed and dried as the others watched. A bell rang. I stepped aside to let all three pass. As the latecomer arced her wadded paper towel over her shoulder into the wastebasket, I knew that I knew her. Or used to.

Sarah Armbruster was a year ahead of me in school. Back when we both lived on Monarch Street, she was the nicest kid around. She taught me to shoot baskets and do back flips. What went wrong?

Okay, so Sarah used to be sweet. That was never true of my ex-step-sister Ronni, and suddenly I was with her again. At *her* school. I wondered if Mr. F's plan was to send me on some kind of scholastic world tour. At least the transitions were painless—just a slight buzz in my head, followed by a whiff of shaved metal.

I recognized Harrison High right away. It was attached to Harrison Middle School, where I did my seventh-grade time while living in Wheeling, West Virginia.

With the attitude of a local celebrity, Ronni stood at the center of a group of animated girls. I checked myself:

still wavy. Nobody here was going to see me. The girls shushed each other and pretended not to notice the hunky guy walking straight toward them. Straight toward me. I did a double take. Cal Wacker looked even handsomer now than he had in Ronni's bedroom, probably because his mouth wasn't oozing bologna sandwich.

"Hey, Ronni," he drawled. "Need a ride home?"

"I guess," she said, sounding like she didn't care. She turned her head so that he couldn't see and gave the girls a knowing grin.

"Later!" they chorused. Ronni didn't answer, just swayed her hips until they moved her toward Cal. I followed. Were we heading for his car? Did Cal Wacker have a car? Could I go along for the ride?

I kept as close to Ronni as I could. In fact, I was so near I could smell her perfume: Tommy Girl, for sure. Good thing she didn't stop without warning, or I would have plowed right into her. Cal's car turned out to be a cherry-red, vintage four-door. A gleaming boat with fins. When he opened the passenger door for Ronni, I shot in ahead of her and hauled myself over the front seat onto a backseat made of shiny white vinyl.

When Cal started the car, my insides started churning. As we rolled forward, I thought I was going to be sick. Most of what I know about science I've learned from *Star Trek*, so I'm no expert on astral-projection. But it felt like my molecular structure was in flux. For a minute, I couldn't even see myself. That made me nervous. Then my stomach settled, my arms and legs came back into focus, and my face shimmered in Cal's rear-view mirror.

Ronni bitched nonstop about her seat adjustment, but Cal didn't seem to mind. He stayed cheerful, as if putting up with constant whining was a normal part of being around Ronni. Which it was.

"I don't see why you're still talking about going to college," she said by way of nothing I could follow. "Look how good you're doing, working right here for my daddy. You think a basketball scholarship is going to make you a man?"

"No. I think a basketball scholarship would make me a basketball player."

"You're already a basketball player. How many years of your life you got to spend doing that?"

"Well, I got to spend the rest of my life being a grown up. Five more years playing basketball sounds about right." He took his eyes off the road long enough to wink at her, but Ronni only huffed. In a whisper Cal added, "I'll be yours till I die, if you'll have me."

Ronni remained unmoved. "I'm not sure you're good enough," she sniffed.

Cal sighed. "You don't want me going away to school, but you don't want me hanging around, neither. Truth is, you don't give a darn about anything till you can't have it."

I wanted to shout, "Ding, ding, ding!" since that summed up the Ronni McWithy I knew and never loved.

"Sometimes you are so thick-headed," she fumed. "You don't need college or basketball! You're already making good money working after school and weekends for my daddy. Think how rich you'll be when you can work for him full-time."

Cal shook his head. "Not much richer. I'm already working thirty hours a week. I need a college degree to get a real career. Working for your daddy's good, but it's just a job."

Which made me wonder what kind of business Short Ron was in. When he and Mom were married, he put every cent they had into a used car dealership that failed. Mom said he dug them in so deep they needed a ladder just to see the grass. Thanks to him, they lost their cars, their furniture, and everything else the creditors could carry away. That was Mom's cue to get a divorce and get us out of there.

Short Ron held onto his house only because it belonged to his mother, who had moved to Detroit long ago and never got around to selling the family home. Short Ron said his mom liked the idea of her only grandchild growing up there. I couldn't believe she'd like anything about her only grandchild.

Ronni's mood didn't improve during the ride home. She told Cal she might change her mind about going to prom with him next month. Three other guys had let her know they'd like her to be their date. She named names.

"I know those guys," Cal said, "and I'm sure they think you're cute. But they'd never try to take my woman. Besides, they already got dates for prom, and they're not the kind to dump a girl at the last minute. Not even for you, baby."

This infuriated Ronni. She opened her door before Cal could pull the car all the way into her driveway, and I knew she'd slam it as soon as she got out. Getting myself out of here might be a whole lot trickier than getting myself in.

No sooner had Ronni bolted than Cal put the car in park and leaped out after her. For a moment, I thought he was going to leave the driver's door open, so I started to slide out behind him. Then he turned back and closed the door. I jerked my leg out of the way just in time. He jogged up the driveway after Ronni, who was already slumped in the back porch glider, clearly in a sulk. Cal never used to fuss that way over me. But I'm not the kind of girl who invites fussing.

Could I get myself out of the car? Staring at the door handle, I wondered if I could move it in my wavy condition. Only one way to find out. I clamped my shimmering fingers on it. Cold—and slightly spongy to the touch. Maybe all hard surfaces felt that way to someone who was astral-projecting. It would explain why the bathroom stall door hadn't hurt. The door creaked ominously as I pushed it open, and it creaked again when I clicked it closed. I held my breath. Cal and Ronnie never looked my way. My wavy feet didn't make crunching sounds on the driveway gravel, and I didn't leave prints. I was there, but not completely there.

On her back porch, Ronni was still whining. Now it was about wanting a different prom dress, which Cal promised to buy. I wanted to scream.

If I did scream, would they hear me? Would I hear myself? I was trying to sort out the rules. Even though I was invisible, I could still feel slight pain, but I didn't think I could bleed. I had no clue if people could smell or feel me. Or if I could operate equipment more complicated than a car door.

I was pondering those issues—and the tranquil blue of Cal's eyes—when something scraped my right shoe. Before I could move, Ronni said, "Look at that stupid cat. He's licking the air like there's food there!"

We all looked, but only one of us saw Rocco eat the egg yolk off my shoe.

Then he rubbed against my leg. We made eye contact, and he held my gaze. This time his fur didn't ruffle, and he made no sound. After a moment, Rocco gave me the cat version of a nod: a slow, calm blink.

chapter six

PARALLEL

Astral-projecting can mess up your sense of time. Suddenly, I was back in the hall at Fowler, between geometry with Mr. Rivera and French with Mme Papinchak. I was walking head-down, trying to dodge egg-lobbers and shovers without bumping into walls, when the floor tilted, and I smelled cooked cabbage. The next thing I knew, I was in our old Atlanta apartment with Wudja circling my head.

Have I mentioned that I hate parrots? Any creature that can get caught in your hair is a sorry excuse for a pet. Mr. F disagrees, but then Mr. F is as bald as a light bulb.

Wudja was on my head, his feet hooked into my scalp, and my host was ignoring the problem. I wondered if Mr. F could see. He never focused his pale eyes on me, even when I swatted at Wudja and made him shriek.

Mr. F said, "So Rocco ate the egg and rubbed your leg and looked at you?"

"And blinked at me," I added.

"You say he's a tuxedo cat," mused Mr. F. "But is he reliable?"

"Tuxedo," cawed Wudja. He lifted off from the crown of my head. "Cat with a wardrobe! Watch out!"

"He's a reliable killer," I said, fanning the air to discourage Wudja from returning. "Mice, rabbits, *birds*—"

"Does he remember you from when you used to live there?" asked Mr. F.

"Maybe. We were never friends."

"Are you willing to work on it?"

Work on making friends with a cat in West Virginia when I had no friends here in Tampa? Not for the first time, I wondered if Mr. F was insane.

"What's your point?" I said.

"Do you want to gain control over your life?"

"What's Rocco got to do with that?"

Instead of answering, Mr. F extended his bony arm as a perch for his parrot. The bird settled. They both studied the ceiling.

"Hello?" I said after a moment. "Why did you bring me here?"

"How's your mother?" said Mr. F.

"Still locked up. And I'm not going back to visit her. She called Trudy last night, so the secret's out. Everyone at Amber Sands will know Nikki Sarno's in the nut house. But she's getting out Saturday. Lucky me."

"How are you—besides lucky?"

I shrugged. "Trudy makes me eat dinner with her every night. She's a better cook than my mom."

"What's new in Muncie, Indiana?" Mr. F said.

"How would I know?"

Wudja hunched down like he was getting ready to fly at my face, so I added, "You mean, with the blonde from the bathroom?"

Mr. F nodded.

"She's running a Girl Mafia. They're after some kid named Amber Reston."

"Why?"

"Because they hate her."

"Why do they hate her?"

"I have no idea."

"Why do the kids at Fowler hate you?"

"I don't know," I began, but then I knew that I did know. "Because I'm not one of them. Because I embarrassed Dustin Yarvich."

"What's going to happen to Amber Reston?"

"How should I know?"

"What's going to happen to Easter Hutton?"

I stared at Mr. F. "What are you saying? There's some kind of parallel?"

"What do you think?"

"Amber-Easter," cawed Wudja. "Easter-Amber."

"What about that girl named Sarah Armbruster?" Mr. Fairless asked.

"What about her?"

"Didn't you like her, once upon a time?"

"Yeah. But now she's part of the Mafia."

"And Rocco is a Serial Killer Cat. Isn't he?"

"So?"

"You said he blinked at you. Are breakthroughs possible?"

I had no answer for that one. Mr. F said, "Could you show Sarah and Rocco that you're there to help?"

"Uh—in case you forgot how this works, only Rocco can see me, and he's a cat."

"Bad cat!" Wudja screeched.

I expected Mr. F to say more, but he didn't. Wudja flapped around the room, cawing, until everything started spinning.

Then I was walking into Mme Papinchak's class, tasting fresh pineapple and speaking flawless French as I apologized for arriving late. I took my seat and kept on talking. My pronunciation sounded so good I could hardly believe my own mouth. The whole class was staring, even Mme Papinchak.

"Très bien, mademoiselle," the teacher said. *"Votre prononciation, c'est magnifique."*

"That's not her, that's Satan talking," muttered a guy in the back of the room. Without turning my head, I recognized the voice of Dustin Yarvich. The class was snickering.

Madame rapped her desk with her pearl-handled gavel.

"Pardonnez-moi, Monsieur? Vous avez une question?"

"No. I mean, *nooooonnn."* Dustin exaggerated the word's nasal sound, and the class giggled.

When the bell rang, students slammed their books and grabbed their bags. Mme Papinchak shouted a reminder that there would be a quiz tomorrow. Most of the class groaned.

"Easter," Madame said as I slipped past her desk. "Could you stay for a moment?"

I wanted to lie and say I had a test next period, but I was pretty sure she knew I had study hall.

"What is it?" I said, my bag over my shoulder. Everyone else was pushing past me. Suddenly, I took a sharp shove in the ribs and cried out in pain.

"Monsieur Yarvich!" Madame shouted. *"Arrêtez-vous!* Stop right there."

Dustin had made it all the way to the door, and I expected him to keep going. But he applied his brakes and slid to a halt.

"What?" he said, looking over his shoulder.

"Come here," Madame said. With a show of disgust, he did. A small crowd was gathering. A few kids who had already exited refilled the doorway. Mme Papinchak made everyone but Dustin and me leave. She closed the door.

"What was that about?" she asked Dustin.

He pretended not to know what she meant.

"Ramming Easter like that. I saw you do it."

"She was blocking the aisle. Not my fault."

"You deliberately rammed her."

"No, I didn't." He tossed his shaggy head. I knew he knew that most girls thought his hair was sexy. "She shouldn't stand in the way like that. She needs to learn."

"Dustin, you need to apologize," Madame said.

I was dying. Didn't she realize what she was doing to me?

"It's okay," I said quickly. "I shouldn't have been in his way."

Dustin looked at me for the first time since she'd called him back, a sly half-grin pulling up one side of his face.

"All right, then." He glanced at Madame. "Hey, I've got to get to chem lab." And he was gone.

Mme Papinchak looked at me. Behind her black-framed glasses, I saw wide, questioning eyes.

"Are you okay?" she asked.

I shook my head and studied the floor. For one awful moment, I was afraid I might cry. I hoped to God she wasn't going to make me explain anything.

"Easter, I handled that all wrong. I am so sorry."

"About what?" I glanced up. Mme Papinchak was pulling on a strand of her hair. She only did that when she was having trouble finding the right word in English. Speaking French never seemed to stump her.

"I stand at the front of this room every day," she said. "Dustin and his sidekicks are making your life miserable."

I wouldn't have given them all the credit, but she was half-right. Then, still tugging at her hair, she gave me some psycho-babble about protecting my sense of self and my personal space, and she reminded me that my guidance counselor was available by appointment.

I kept nodding and inching toward the door. When I finally got there, she added, "Oh, I almost forgot. I wanted to tell you that you've made excellent progress in this class since you arrived. Today, especially. You seem to have a real feel for the language."

I wasn't about to admit that I really liked French and had been spending extra time on my homework. It came easily to me, which was more than I could say for any other subject.

For the rest of the day, I kept an even lower profile than usual. After my last class, I followed my new routine of hiding out in the library until almost every student had gone home. I was anxious about getting online to talk to Andrew. Although I didn't feel ready to tell him about Mr. F and the astral-projections, I needed his advice about my mom.

While waiting for an available computer, I decided to tackle my geometry homework. At the end of class, Mr. Rivera had given us a handout. This is how it began:

> You may have questions about parallel lines and their purposes. Understanding them can help you solve problems.

I inhaled sharply. Did everyone get this handout? Or could this be the work of Mr. Fairless? I read on.

> Two lines are parallel if they share a plane but never intersect. Parallel lines can be said to have the same tendency. *Easter Hutton is parallel to Amber Reston.*
>
> Two lines are perpendicular if they intersect at a right angle. Perpendicular lines can be said to

> occur in opposition. *Easter Hutton is perpendicular to Ronni McWithy.*

I blinked. The italicized sentences disappeared.

In geometry class the next day, we reviewed the handout. Everyone had a copy, but I was the only student paying attention.

chapter seven

INTERSECTING

If Mr. Rivera was supposed to be Mr. F's messenger at Fowler, he wasn't very good at it. Nothing he said about parallels or perpendiculars helped me make sense of my life. When he started talking about intersecting planes, I zoned out until the bell rang.

Mme Papinchak was waiting for me in the hall outside French class. She pressed a folded piece of paper into my hand and whispered, "This is urgent."

Typed on school letterhead I read:

See me *immediately.*
–Dr. Hui

When I glanced up, Madame nodded then shook her head. I think she was trying to tell me *yes*, I needed to go now, and *no*, she hadn't arranged this.

Dr. Hui, guidance counselor, turned out to be a woman who didn't look much older than the students she was hired to help. When she stood up to greet me, we were exactly the same height: five foot two. No wonder she chose a job where she could sit behind a desk all day. In front of a class, kids my age would crush her.

"The reason for our meeting is your mother." Dr. Hui believed in getting right to the point.

My stomach clenched. "Is she all right?"

"She's hospitalized. You knew that, right?"

I nodded. What planet did she think I lived on?

"She's getting out tomorrow," I said. "Or did that change?"

Dr. Hui had no information about that. Apparently, that wasn't why I was in her office.

"Hillsborough County Children's Services contacted me. It has come to their attention that you're an unsupervised minor. They need to know who's in charge of you, and where."

I wanted to say, "Well, there's this blind bald guy with a parrot who zaps me between Tampa, Atlanta, Wheeling, and Muncie . . ."

Instead I said, "Our next-door neighbor."

Dr. Hui wrote down Trudy's full name, address, and phone number.

"Who reported me?" I said.

"I don't think anyone 'reported' you. Presumably your mother listed you as next of kin when she was admitted." Dr. Hui peered at me over her glasses. "Are you doing all right?"

"I come to school, don't I?"

That sounded a little ruder than necessary, so I added, "If I was a mess, do you think I'd get my butt over here every day?"

For the first time, Dr. Hui smiled. At least I think she did. The expression came and went so fast I wasn't sure. Then she rearranged her papers.

"It says here that you have no family other than your mother. Is that true?"

"Basically."

"No father?"

"Not anymore."

"What does that mean, Easter?"

"It means we think he moved to Mexico when I was twelve, but we never heard from him again." I took a deep breath. "He was a junkie, okay? My mom threw him out, and last we heard, he was crossing the border."

Dr. Hui looked at me a long time without blinking. Then she said, "You're angry at both your parents, aren't you?"

"I'm angry in general. Life mostly sucks."

"No."

"No?" I gave her my most amazed expression. "What planet do you live on?"

"The one I shape and reshape every day. We create our own world within the larger human experience. It's called our frame of reference, and it's the only world that counts."

I almost laughed. "Dustin Yarvich and his friends make fun of me and shove me and throw raw eggs at me. But that's their world, right? So it's not my problem?"

A crease appeared between Dr. Hui's thin eyebrows. "Is that going on here at Fowler?"

"At the Fowler in my frame of reference it is."

I couldn't believe I'd said that. To a school official no less. Someone with a real office and the letters Ph.D. after her name. I wanted to call the words back, but as Andrew used to say, "You can't un-ring a bell."

Which reminded me that I needed my best friend now more than ever. It had been five days since he'd emailed me, and I was getting worried. It wasn't like Andrew to leave my messages unanswered.

Dr. Hui tore a page from the pad she was writing on and handed it to me. It looked like a prescription.

"What's this?" I said.

"A reminder of your next appointment. We're going to talk again."

"We are?"

Then she ordered me back to Mme Papinchak's class and turned her attention to her computer.

Fortunately, Madame was playing some stupid black-and-white all-in-French movie with no subtitles. Most of the class was asleep. I put my head down on my desk and pretended to be invisible.

Dustin Yarvich hissed, "You missed the quiz, Hutton. Maybe Papinchak will let you translate the movie instead."

Madame heard that and paused the VCR. In French she asked Monsieur Yarvich if he had a question.

He grunted, *"Non."*

Then she glanced from me to Dustin to me again like she was trying to decide whether to turn this into a lesson. Mentally I begged her to let everybody go back to sleep. *Mais non.*

"Mademoiselle Hutton, would you oblige the class and translate the rest of this scene?"

I politely declined in French and laid my head back down on my desk.

"As Monsieur suggested, it can be your way of making up the quiz."

I stared at her through one open eye.

She added, "Just three minutes. You can do it. I'm sure you can."

It was suddenly so still, you could have heard a bird breathe. Something about the way Madame spoke made me think she might actually know what she was doing. And so might I.

I sat up straight and cleared my throat. She released the pause button on the VCR and then stepped back.

We were in the middle of a scene between an old man and a young woman. He might have been her grandfather because he was giving her a lot of advice. She just sat there listening as he talked about courage and honor and honesty. He ended the scene with these words:

"Reach beyond yourself and use parts of yourself that you never knew you had. Most important, my dear, believe that anything can happen. Because, truly, anything can."

"Très bien," Madame said, hitting the pause button again. "We'll watch the rest of the movie now and discuss it on Monday."

When she restarted the tape, I could feel everybody's eyes still on me, including Mme Papinchak's, behind her black glasses. At least the room stayed quiet.

At the end of the hour, I managed to slip out the door ahead of everybody. I kept my head down the rest of the day. Following my translation in French class, plus what

I'd confessed to Dr. Hui, I expected Dustin and company to descend on me like a swarm of black flies. But nothing happened.

In the school library after my last class, I parked myself in front of the first available computer. Andrew wasn't online, and he hadn't emailed me, either. My already low spirits sagged again. I wondered if something was bothering him. Maybe I should call him collect to find out. Andrew's parents rarely answered the phone at night. If he took the call, he'd accept the charges, and then we could talk for hours. Provided nobody else needed to use the pay phone at the Amber Sands Clubhouse. That was the only place I could call from at night, besides Trudy's. No way I'd attempt a private conversation inside the Tin Daisy. Even if Trudy let me tie up her phone, she'd hover, overhearing every word on both ends.

Suddenly my message center beeped to announced that aseaforth@freeair.net was online. I typed:

> HEY, ANDREW!!!!! DON'T EVER NEGLECT ME LIKE THAT AGAIN, OR—SO HELP ME—I'LL TELL YOUR MOTHER ABOUT THE TIME YOU WORE HER PAISLEY SILK BLOUSE TO SCHOOL!

I held my breath for his reply and was surprised when it didn't come. I waited like five minutes, but nothing happened. I was just starting to type a second message when this filled my IM box:

Dear out_there_girl@noway.com,
We don't know who you are, but we assume that you're a friend of Andrew's. This is his mother and father. Ordinarily we would never interfere with Andrew's privacy, but as you may know, he's in deep trouble, and we're trying to save him. We hope you can help.

chapter eight
MISSING

I could picture Mr. and Mrs. Seaforth hunched over Andrew's computer at the red lacquer desk in his bedroom under the poster of Keanu Reeves. They probably thought Andrew bought it because he admired Keanu's acting. But I wasn't tracking that line of thought just then; I had turned clammy with alarm.

Andrew was not the kind of person who gets into "deep trouble." What did that mean? And why did he need to be "saved"? I couldn't imagine how I could help from here, but I had to try. If I told his parents my real name, I was pretty sure they'd remember me since I used to hang around their house now and then, playing computer games with Andrew in his room. We always left the door wide open, but I thought his parents secretly hoped we would close it and start making out. Not that I was their ideal choice of a girlfriend. They just wanted their son to be straight so badly that any female would do.

Before replying, I took a deep breath. My hands were shaking, but I managed to type:

> I'M EASTER HUTTON, AND I LIVE IN TAMPA NOW. ANDREW AND I INSTANT-MESSAGE EACH OTHER, BUT I HAVEN'T HEARD FROM HIM LATELY. WHAT'S GOING ON?

When they didn't reply right away, I wondered what hair color they were picturing me with. The first time we met it was sapphire. After that I tried turquoise, purple, and maroon. Now it was flat black, which made a statement about the way I saw the world. I imagined Mr. and Mrs. Seaforth, who are like fifty years old, asking each other if they really wanted to get the girl with the nose stud involved.

Andrew's mom and my mom were about as different as two mothers could be. Mrs. Seaforth was one of those busy professional women who almost missed having kids. Her job was running the laboratory at Coca-Cola. Who knew they even needed a lab at a soft-drink company? I mean, why mess with the formula? I asked Andrew if that meant we should expect some liter bottles to taste better than others, like the way my mom's spaghetti sauce never turned out the same way twice. But he said no, it's about quality control, making sure you got the same taste experience every single time.

Mrs. Seaforth built her career first and her family second. But she was determined to be as good a mom as she was a chemist. According to Andrew, she read every book ever written on parenting and took notes on his development like it was a science project. Not that she treated him like a lab rat, just that she was passionate about the process even though she was almost too old for the job. Whenever Mrs. Seaforth was with her son, she glowed with love and pride and hope all mixed together. It was like she knew he was really special. I used to wish my mom would look at me the way Mrs. Seaforth looked at Andrew.

Mr. Seaforth was nice, too, but very quiet. He was one of those types who always seems to be thinking something important but rarely says anything at all. Mr. Seaforth worked from home doing boring data analysis for an insurance company. Although he was usually shut up in his office next to the kitchen, sometimes he would come out and say hi when he heard Andrew and me getting ourselves something to eat. Mr. Seaforth would watch Andrew closely, like his son might be on the verge of doing something miraculous. Maybe like kissing me. Of course that never happened.

I remembered all this as a way of distracting myself from how long Andrew's parents were taking to reply. Finally they wrote back:

> Of course we remember you, Easter. Your hair color was the most interesting of all Andrew's friends. I thought the maroon was especially flattering.
>
> As for our son—we're trying to find him. Did Andrew ever mention someone named Marco to you?

I gulped. Would I be betraying Andrew if I let his parents know about Marco? As far as I knew, Marco was still in the closet, and Andrew's parents weren't ready to accept that their son was permanently gay. Then again, this was probably a real emergency. So I wrote the truth:

> I don't know Marco's last name or where he lives. He doesn't go to our school, I mean the school Andrew goes to. I think he attends some private academy. I never met him, but Andrew said he was special. Smart, too. He speaks like three languages.

I hoped that last part would relieve their minds. At least Andrew hadn't hooked up with some high school dropout.

Several minutes ticked by. When Mr. and Mrs. Seaforth still hadn't replied, I nervously typed:

> CAN YOU TELL ME WHAT'S GOING ON? I'M REALLY WORRIED.

Apparently, the Seaforths had lost track of me while they discussed the situation. Andrew's mother wrote

> SORRY, EASTER. THIS IS HARD TO EXPLAIN, BUT WE'RE WONDERING WHAT YOU KNOW ABOUT ANDREW'S SPECIAL GIFT?

Special gift? My mind raced. It didn't seem likely that Mr. and Mrs. Seaforth had suddenly decided being gay was a good thing. Cautiously I typed

> I'M NOT SURE WHAT YOU MEAN.

Mrs. Seaforth replied

> ANDREW IS WHAT'S KNOWN AS A "POST-COGNITIVE READER." WE FIRST NOTICED HIS GIFT WHEN HE WAS FOUR YEARS OLD. I'VE KEPT CAREFUL NOTES SINCE THEN. IN CERTAIN PEOPLE, ANDREW CAN DETECT PIECES OF THEIR PAST AND KNOW THINGS ABOUT THEM THAT THEY MAY NOT EVEN REMEMBER THEMSELVES.

I gasped, suddenly recalling a night when I had dinner with Andrew and his parents. Andrew was going on and on about how smart I was. I figured he was doing it to distract his parents from my currently turquoise hair. To make me seem more acceptable. Anyhow, I was getting embarrassed. I told him—and his parents—that I wasn't that bright, and I tried to change the subject. But Andrew was stubborn. He said, "How can you say you're not smart? You came in second, two years in a row, in the Delaware County Spelling Bee!"

That was weird for two reasons:

1. Andrew didn't know me when I lived in Delaware County (Muncie), Indiana, and
2. I had never told him—or anyone in Atlanta—about being in a Spelling Bee, let alone almost winning two of them.

Was that an example of a post-cognitive reading? I fired off the question to Mrs. Seaforth. She instantly answered:

> YES! WE'VE ALWAYS WORRIED THAT ANDREW MIGHT GET IN TROUBLE FOR KNOWING THE WRONG THING ABOUT THE WRONG PERSON. USUALLY, THE FIRST THING HE CAN "READ" IS SOMEONE'S MOST EMBARRASSING OR MOST FRIGHTENING MEMORY. AS HE GETS TO KNOW A PERSON BETTER, HE PICKS UP ALL KINDS OF FACTS ABOUT THEIR PAST. BUT YOU KNOW ANDREW. HE RESPECTS OTHER PEOPLE. HE CAN KEEP THEIR SECRETS.

I gulped. The Delaware County Spelling Bee wasn't my worst memory by any means. Andrew must have decided not to comment on the traumatic stuff he'd "read" in me—

like my memories of my parents' breakup. Mrs. Seaforth continued:

> Here's what happened: Andrew was acting strange all week. Not eating, not talking, not looking or acting like himself. When he failed to come home from school by 5:00 yesterday, we called the office and learned that he'd been absent all week. We don't know where he's been going or where he is now. He hasn't contacted us. And that's not like Andrew.

She was right. I shivered, having personal experience with disappearing, or at least with being invisible. For a moment, I wondered if Andrew could also astral-project. Maybe our wavy selves would wind up in the same place at the same time! *Intersecting*, as Mr. Rivera called it. Then I remembered that I don't go missing when I go "elsewhere." I just look vacant.

Suddenly I recalled something else. When Andrew last messaged me, he said he thought he knew things about Marco that Marco wasn't yet ready to discuss. What if Marco was responsible for Andrew's disappearance?

The Seaforths were typing another message:

> The police said we should try to remember everything Andrew mentioned in recent weeks. We knew he had a new friend named Marco, but we didn't meet him. In fact, we thought they'd stopped seeing each other.

Andrew got upset last week about a gay bashing that was reported on the evening news. We were concerned about the incident, too, since it involved a young man Andrew's age. Did he mention it to you?

I replied truthfully that he hadn't. But cold new fears were forming in my gut. Andrew suddenly seemed so vulnerable.

The Seaforths thanked me for my cooperation and invited me to call collect anytime day or night if I thought of something else. Mrs. Seaforth even gave me her work and cell phone numbers. Then she added:

I never met your mother, Easter, but she must have raised you right. You're a true and caring friend. Andrew thinks the world of you. This I know.

Through hot tears I peered at the pewter armor ring Andrew gave me, remembering how he promised that his friendship would always protect me.

If only I could make that work both ways.

Mrs. Seaforth said she hoped I was happy living in Florida. I wish. Trudging back to Amber Sands Estates in the blinding late afternoon sun, I felt like an ant frying under a malicious kid's magnifying glass. And not just because of the white-bright heat. Everything that mattered to me was smoldering in one big bonfire: My mom had lost her mind as well as her baby, I was taking orders from a blind man who thought I was his cosmic hand puppet, the kids in my new school were using me for target practice, and now my best friend had disappeared.

Just when I thought the smoke couldn't get any thicker, Trudy met me at the door of the Tin Daisy with the worst news yet:

"Easter, dear, the hospital called. Your mother seems to be missing."

chapter nine
NINETEEN

"What do you mean, she's *missing?"* I said. "Mom was in lockdown. In the loony bin."

Trudy nodded. "That's what I told the lady who called! Only I didn't say 'loony bin.' She said Nikki was with a group on a supervised walk—and then she wasn't."

"You mean they lost her?"

"More like she lost them. They think she made a break for it."

Mom never was one for following rules. But she was due to come home the next morning. Why couldn't she hang in there just one more day? If she had run away, where had she run to? And why hadn't she come to see me?

Trudy said, "She'll probably call here tonight. Or, better yet, show up at the door. I'll bet she wants to surprise you."

Mom had a knack for doing that, all right. Usually not in a good way.

Trudy seemed pretty calm, and that surprised me. It didn't take much to get her worked up. Whenever I was late coming home from school, or if I refused to talk about my day, she would start banging around the Tin Daisy's tiny kitchen, opening and closing the only two cupboards she had. Which made *me* nervous. When you think about it, Mom's vanishing act was bad news for Trudy, too. She would have to keep an eye on me until Mom turned up. Now that Dr. Hui was involved, Hillsborough County Children's Services would probably make a house call.

Just then the phone rang. Trudy smiled at me nervously. I could tell she was hoping as hard as I was that it was my mom.

"Hellooo?" She answered in a way that sounded like the first notes of a song. Instantly her smile fell, and she turned her head away. I heard her murmur, "Oh dear! Are you sure?"

Then she lowered her voice until I couldn't hear what she was saying, but she seemed to be repeating what she was told. I picked out a few phrases, none of them reassuring: "left a note . . . family in north Georgia . . . notified the police."

As soon as she hung up, I said, "That was about my mom, wasn't it?"

Trudy moistened her crinkly lips. "Easter, dear, there's been . . . a development."

"What happened? Is Mom hurt?"

"No, no. She's fine, as far as we know. But it appears that she ran off . . . with a young man."

"What?!"

"A young man from the hospital. She left a note—"

"Mom ran off with a mental case?!" I cried.

"No, dear, not a mental case. A janitor. She ran off with a janitor. He's nineteen."

"Nineteen?!"

Mom was thirty-four. I was freaking out.

"They found a note addressed to you in Nikki's room. Your mom didn't want you to worry—"

I clapped both hands over my face and fell over sideways in the yellow vinyl armchair.

"Now, now," said Trudy. She was probably afraid I was going to start crying. I was way past crying.

"My mom left me here and ran off with a guy who's nineteen," I said dully. "What am I supposed to do? What does she think will happen to me?"

"I'm sure she's working that out, dear." But Trudy's shaky voice suggested that she was thinking what I was thinking: my mom had dumped me.

"You said something about the police," I mumbled through my fingers.

"The hospital notified the police that your mother's missing, and the janitor, too. He walked off the job."

"What was that about family in north Georgia?"

"Oh—the janitor just moved to Florida, so the hospital thinks maybe he went back home. He's from Dalton. Isn't that where carpets come from?"

I didn't know anything about carpets, but I sat up straight. Maybe my mom wasn't in lust with the dude. More likely she was using him for a free ride back to James Dean Bakeman.

Trudy lumbered off to the mini-bathroom in the back of the trailer. If Mom really was en route to Atlanta, I would give anything to go, too—not only because I hated being here, but because Andrew was in Atlanta. Or, to be accurate, Andrew had gone missing in Atlanta. If I could go back there, maybe I could help find him.

The phone rang. Since Trudy was still in the bathroom, I grabbed it on the first ring.

"Easter? Oh, my God, is that you?"

Despite a roar of static, I recognized my mom's voice.

"Where are you?" I cried.

"Oh, babe, did I worry you?"

"Mom, what's going on?"

A long rumble of static followed. I asked her again where she was and thought she said Bob's Good Garage.

"Isn't that where we left our car?" I shouted.

The noise was so bad I wondered if she'd disconnected. Then she said, "—and it's so sweet of Roger to help pay the bill!"

"Who's Roger?" I yelled.

The noise stopped so suddenly that I heard my voice echoing "Roger-er-er" on the line.

"Hello?" I said. "Mom, are you there?"

"I'm here. But I've got to run. Don't worry. Roger's a very good driver."

"Take me with you!" I shouted even though our connection was now clear.

Mom gasped as if my request shocked her. "Oh, Easter—didn't you hear what I said? We're on our way to get you right now. Roger's father is dying in Dalton, so we made a deal: he helped pay the bill on our Taurus in exchange for a ride north. We'll be in Atlanta before midnight!"

chapter ten
DREAMING

I must have whooped with joy. Trudy burst out of the bathroom still adjusting the elastic waistband on her red stretch pants.

"What is it? What happened?" she demanded.

That was when I realized I was crying. Big fat tears of relief were rolling down my cheeks.

"We're going back to Atlanta!" I was so happy that I gave Trudy a hug. And I am not a person who hugs. But this was a special occasion, like Christmas and graduation day rolled into one.

Trudy was totally baffled, even after I explained it to her three times. Finally, I said I had to get packed. Back in our sorry trailer, I was throwing stuff into my backpack and duffel bag when I heard a familiar horn honking. The Taurus rolls again! Dropping everything, I flung open the squeaky screen door. There was Mom, leaning out the passenger-side window of our beat-up blue car.

"Come on!" she yelled. "We've got to hit the road!"

"But you're not packed," I said.

"No time. I'll get what I need later."

"But *I'm* still packing."

"Zip it up, and let's go! Roger's daddy may not make it through the night."

"But—" I stared at her. We'd moved here a month ago. No way I could gather up my whole life in five minutes.

"Move your ass!" Mom roared. "If you're worried about leaving something behind, get over it!"

She was giving me one of her dark looks. Since she'd just escaped from the nut house, it seemed unwise to provoke her. I groaned loudly, went back inside, and crammed a few more clothes and CDs into my bags. The horn honked again. I swore under my breath, heaved one bag over each shoulder, and let the door slam behind me.

"Lock up!" Mom ordered.

I wanted to ask what for. If she didn't care about packing her stuff, she shouldn't care about locking it up. But I gritted my teeth and did what I was told. When I turned around again, Trudy was leaning on the car, talking to Mom. They both looked at me when I came over.

"Easter's a good girl," Trudy said, giving me a big smile that wasn't fake.

"Sometimes," Mom sighed. "Thanks for everything. We'll be in touch."

I gave Trudy the trailer key and climbed in. My first view of Roger with the dying father in Dalton was the back of his head. And a very nice view it was, with longish, wavy dark hair that looked clean and healthy. I could smell his sandalwood shampoo when I slid in behind him. Then he turned around, and the view got better—smiling brown eyes and a square jaw with a stubble of beard.

"Hey, Easter. Nice to meet you." The voice rumbled with a warm Southern accent. He gave me his hand to shake.

"Sorry about the honking," he added with a wink. "Your mama made me do it. She's a little over-excited about us getting on the road."

It turned out that Roger had a way of calming Mom down. By the time we'd turned onto I-275, she'd settled back in her seat and started singing along with the radio. Not once on the whole trip did she question the way Roger drove, not even his speed or his left-hand turns. She also liked his music, his stories, and his politics. But I knew my mom well enough to know that Roger was just a means to an end. He had a Georgia emergency, and so did she. He needed reliable transportation, and she could provide it—if he could help pay for it.

I imagined Mom's plan: to confront James Dean Bakeman and demand that he treat her right. Baby or not, it was time for him to make good on his promise that he'd get divorced and marry her. He also needed to cough up some cash. Mom wouldn't take no, or even "later," for an answer anymore.

As the sun set and the miles rolled by, Roger and Mom took turns telling me the story of how they "busted her out."

"The first time I laid eyes on this guy, I knew I could trust him," Mom said. "And that never happens to me. I have such bad luck."

I wanted to point out the connection between having no trust in a man and having bad luck with him, but Mom rushed on with her story.

"When Roger was cleaning the TV room the second day I was there, I told him about losing my baby. He listened, just as sweet as could be, and said he understood because his mama lost a baby, and it made her crazy, too."

"She cried for a whole month," Roger piped up.

"After that, we talked every day," Mom said, smiling at her driver. "Roger told me about his daddy dying of lung cancer up in Dalton."

"Then Nikki mentioned that this here car was gathering dust over at Bob's Good Garage," Roger said. "So we made a deal and a plan. I'd help cover costs, and we'd both get our butts out of Tampa. Nikki said she'd fall behind her group on their two o'clock walk, and I said I'd skip cleaning the fifth floor restrooms. By two-thirty, we'd meet up at the hospital cab stand. And we did! We had a good laugh about it, too—both of us AWOL, waiting in plain sight to catch a cab to our getaway car!"

Seeing Mom smile made me smile. I started to relax. Tampa was getting farther away by the minute. Just south of Valdosta, I must have dozed off.

I dreamed I went back to our old apartment in Atlanta—the conventional way, not by being zapped. I walked into the yellow brick building, just like I used to. The foyer was still that ugly shade of lime green, some of the fluorescent hall lights were still flickering, and the metal door to our unit still had a big dent in it where, once upon a time, somebody had tried to kick it in. When I knocked, nobody answered, so I turned the knob. To my surprise, the door swung open. Inside, the furniture was rearranged exactly as Mr. Fairless now has it. Otherwise there was no sign of him or of anyone. The window was wide open, a refreshing breeze making the tan curtains dance. Suddenly I heard Wudja cawing and turned in time to see him fly straight at my head. I ducked, and the parrot kept right on going, out through the open window into the bright clear sky. I watched until he was a distant speck.

Then the breeze became a wind, and I heard paper rattling. Pages from a newspaper were blowing around the apartment. I closed the window and scooped them up. One headline caught my eye: *Help Find Missing Teen*. I sat down on our old couch in its new location to read:

> *Andrew Seaforth, 16, a sophomore at Claymore High School, was reported missing on Thursday. His parents, though older than normal, are working tirelessly to find him. They released this list of possible clues in the hopes that others will join in the search for their son, who is a truly wonderful human being and the only friend of Easter Hutton.*
>
> *Andrew had a new friend named Marco, who attends private school and speaks several languages.*
>
> *Andrew was concerned about a recent gay-bashing incident that involved someone his own age.*
>
> *Andrew once mentioned the term Homefree. It is not known whether this is a place, a political movement, or an organization devoted to (story continued on page 18)*

Except there was no page 18, at least not among the pieces of paper I'd picked up. I searched the apartment for the missing page, peering under chairs and in corners. Suddenly there was a violent *thunk* at the window. I looked up in time to see Wudja bounce off the glass, hang in mid-air for an instant like a broken green and yellow feather duster, and then drop from sight.

My own cry of alarm woke me. That, and the taste of fresh pineapple.

"You all right back there?" Mom asked sleepily.

"Bad dream," I mumbled. Or was it?

chapter eleven

SHOWTIME

"Easter—wake up. We're here." I must have fallen back asleep. Mom was shaking me awake, her voice urgent.

"We're in Atlanta?" I asked fuzzily.

"Right. And you're coming in with me."

I uncurled from my fetal position on the back seat, where I was using my pack for a pillow.

"In where?" I yawned.

When I looked out the window, I knew. With a sudden spike of dread, I grasped the full scope of Mom's plan.

"Oh, no—" I began. She cut me off.

"Easter, I don't have the time or energy to listen to you whine. Come with me, and don't say a word unless I ask you to, got it?"

"But—"

"Don't argue with me!"

"Easy now, Nikki," said a voice as cool and soothing as chocolate syrup. That's when I remembered that Roger was with us. Roger was *still* with us. I was pretty sure that was a good thing although I didn't have a clue what role he'd play now. From the set of Mom's jaw, I knew this was no time to ask.

Roger got out of the car and walked around it to open Mom's door. Then he opened my door. I don't think anyone's ever done that for me, not since I was too little to open it for myself. Mom didn't say thanks, but I did.

Roger said, "You're very welcome."

Stiffly I stepped out of the car. It must have rained earlier. The blacktop surface of the parking lot was shiny wet, the puddles reflecting a sign so familiar I could easily read it backwards and upside down: Magnolia Diner. The words glowed in flowing white and yellow neon script. Besides ours, there were about twenty cars under the humming yellow security lights. The Magnolia Diner was catching the after-movie crowd. Mom would have an emotionally primed audience for her dramatic presentation.

We moved as a unit toward the front door, passing James Dean Bakeman's silver Sebring convertible. I felt like I was inside one of those actor's nightmares, where you're about to go onstage, but you don't know your lines or even the name of the play you're in. I wondered if Roger knew his part. He looked amazingly alert and handsome after all those hours at the wheel. Maybe he sensed my anxiety. When he held the door open, our eyes met, and he winked.

Mom had already marched past us straight up to the hostess stand. I heard her say, "Hi, Arlene. How ya doing? Go get James Dean for me, will you."

I couldn't hear what Arlene said back, but it must have been the wrong answer. Mom's voice came again, louder.

"I don't care how busy he is. Go get him. I just drove four hundred and fifty-nine miles to see his sorry face."

Arlene shuffled away, shaking her salt-and-pepper head. Mom was standing, arms akimbo, directly beneath a huge hanging lamp. It provided a perfect circle of pure white light. The crowd at the Magnolia Diner didn't know it yet, but the evening's main entertainment was about to begin.

"We're supposed to stand right behind her," Roger whispered to me. "Remember, it's her show."

He actually used the word "show." That relaxed me a little because it meant he knew what we were in for, and even so, he was prepared to stay.

"What about your father? I thought you were in a hurry to see him," I whispered back.

"I'm going there next," Roger said. "Gotta take care of things one at a time."

Maybe that was my whole problem in life. I felt like I was trying to handle about fifty things at once, the result being that everything was always out of control.

Roger placed a hand at the center of my back and gently guided me into position. His touch made me feel secure and kind of sexy. I took a deep breath. The diner smelled like chicken-fried steak and mashed potatoes with country gravy, which reminded me that all I'd eaten since leaving Florida was a couple bags of chips. Not that hunger was my biggest problem. I stared straight ahead at the cash register and concentrated on getting through the next few minutes. It was kind of like being at the dentist—you know it's going to hurt, but you have to do it, and then you can go home. Only I wasn't sure where tonight's "home" would turn out to be.

The next thing I knew, James Dean Bakeman was standing before us.

"Nikki!" he exclaimed in a voice that sounded breathy and secretive. "What the deuce are you doing here?"

"We have a problem, James Dean," Mom said. Her voice was weirdly calm and clear.

"Let's step outside and discuss it," he replied, starting toward the door.

"Oh, no." Mom's voice rang out like a song. "We're going to discuss it right here. Right in front of your staff and your customers. You're not making me and my daughter go anywhere ever again."

"Nikki, please." James Dean Bakeman tried to take Mom by the arm. She sidestepped him without leaving her circle of light.

"You're the father of my unborn child, and you promised to marry me."

Suddenly the entire restaurant was silent. I imagined all those mouths full of mashed potatoes or maybe strawberry pie stopping in mid-chew.

"You sent me and my daughter off to a trailer park in Tampa so that you could get a divorce. We haven't heard from you in a *month.* Or received one dime of assistance. You abandoned us!"

James Dean Bakeman's piggy little eyes swept across the restaurant. Beads of sweat glistened on his high forehead. He cleared his throat.

"This is neither the time nor the place—"

"You're out of time," Mom said, her voice loud enough to reach even the far corner booth. "Your past just caught up to you."

"Oh yeah?" James Dean took a step back and glanced from Mom to me to Roger. "Who's he?"

"Roger Lee Trueblood of Dalton, Georgia." The former janitor extended his hand, but James Dean didn't take it. "I'm a personal friend of these ladies, and I can vouch for the fact that they're in distress. If you're half the man you've told them you are, then you'll do right by them, starting here and now."

"Or what? Are you threatening me, boy?" James Dean Bakeman inflated his stocky physique to its full height, which wasn't impressive next to Roger.

"No sir, I am not," replied our driver. "But your behavior's causing big problems for this mother and daughter. I'm here to make sure their issues are resolved."

James Dean Bakeman worked his eyebrows like knitting needles. I figured he was mentally wrestling with a couple nasty alternatives: give Mom some cash or try to throw her out. He stunned me by saying in a loud, mean voice, "The boy's a little young for you, isn't he, Nikki? Then again, you never were particular about your men."

A soft whoosh rattled the air as the diner audience gasped.

I held my breath, prepared for a classic Nikki Sarno explosion. But Mom's retort was as calm as the sweetest summer day.

"I guess I was never particular enough, given that I spent time with *you.* Then again, you were never particular about the fact that you were married. How many waitresses have you fooled around with, James Dean? I should think by now your wife would be delighted to give you that divorce."

James Dean Bakeman narrowed his tiny eyes until they were slits. "Get help, Nikki, for your daughter's sake, before you mess her up more than you already have. Just look at the girl."

I felt everybody in the diner do exactly as he said. There was a chorus of murmurs as they evaluated the mess that was me. James Dean shook his head and started toward his office.

"What about *your* daughter? The one I'm carrying in my womb?" Mom cried out.

You could have heard butter melting, the diner was so still. Leave it to Mom to lie for what she wanted and to make a spectacle of herself in the process. But James Dean Bakeman didn't glance back. He just kept on walking.

"You owe me!" shouted Mom.

With that, Roger flew into action. He rushed after James Dean, grabbed him by the shoulder, and spun him around.

"You heard the lady," Roger said. "You got her pregnant, and now you owe her support. It's the least you can do, sir."

"I owe her nothing!" James Dean Bakeman hissed. "She's a nutcase. She should be locked away somewhere!"

Still gripping James Dean's shoulder, Roger leaned in so close that I could no longer see our driver's face. After a moment, I realized he was whispering something in James Dean's ear. Whatever it was took a long time to say. I watched James Dean's expression shift from rage to concentration to resignation. Finally, he nodded once and motioned curtly for Roger to follow him. They headed toward James Dean's office.

"We'll wait outside," Mom announced with dignity. I scrambled after her through the front door.

"What do you think you're doing?" I demanded.

"Making sure we're provided for." Mom was lighting a cigarette. Next she'd probably want a beer. Now that there was no more baby, she felt free to resume her bad habits.

"You expect James Dean to marry you after *that?*" I asked.

"Who on earth wants to marry James Dean?" She inhaled deeply.

"You did—"

"That was then, this is now. Things have changed, Easter, in case you failed to notice."

I blinked at her. "You lied in there. You told him you were pregnant."

"A woman does what a woman's got to do. Someday you'll figure that out."

We leaned against the car in silence, Mom smoking, me listening to my stomach rumble. A young couple came out of the diner and walked past us on their way to their car.

"I wouldn't eat there again if I were you," Mom advised them. "The cook's crazy. He spits on every meal. The manager's too scared to fire him."

Mom smoked a second cigarette, then a third. I sneaked a peek at her watch. It was twenty past midnight.

"What's Roger doing in there?" I asked.

"You'll see," she said.

Since the Magnolia Diner is always open, people continued to come and go. Mom warned them all about the crazy cook who likes to spit. One couple actually got back in their car and went someplace else to eat. Mom enjoyed a good laugh.

Then Roger was loping toward us, waving something in his hand. He gave it to Mom and opened her car door. Next he opened mine.

When I got in, I peered over Mom's shoulder. In the dim overhead light, she was unzipping a dark green vinyl pouch about the size of a thick business envelope. From it she withdrew what looked like a stack of hundred-dollar bills.

"I counted it myself," Roger said. He closed his door, and the overhead light clicked off. Instantly he flipped it back on so that Mom could see her money.

"Did we get what we wanted?" she asked, fanning out the stack.

"Twenty-five hundred in cash, and there's a check for the rest," Roger said. "You cash that at Southern Savings Bank first thing in the morning, y'hear. If there's a problem, I promised Mr. Bakeman I'd come down from Dalton to visit him and his family."

Mom was quiet for a long time—not counting the bills, just staring at them spread out on her lap.

Finally she said, "You're more of a man at nineteen than most men ever are."

With both hands, Mom reached over and turned Roger's head toward her, even though he was driving. The money tumbled on the floor as she kissed him hard on the mouth.

I felt a flash of heat. What she'd said was true. But I wanted to be the one to say it, and the one to thank him properly. After all, Roger Lee Trueblood had protected me, too. And nineteen's a whole lot closer to sixteen than it is to thirty-four.

chapter twelve
COOKIE'S

Only after I recovered from watching Mom kiss Roger did it hit me—Where were we going to sleep tonight? It was almost one in the morning, and no one had mentioned getting a room.

Before I could ask, Mom announced, "I'm going to ride along to Dalton with Roger—to help his family in their hour of need."

I stared at her. "What about me?"

Mom sighed. "Easter, why must you always be so selfish? Can't you think of a single friend from school you could stay with for a few days?"

I started to remind her that it was the middle of the night, but she cut me off. "You have a place to stay tonight. I made sure of that. But I might be gone a few days, and Cookie can only keep you one night. Her sister's family moved in with her, so it's crowded."

Once again Mom was dumping me on someone else. Ordinarily, I would have wanted to explode. But Cookie happened to be our former neighbor, a chain-smoking stripper who lived one floor below our old apartment.

One floor below Mr. F and Wudja. If Mr. F and Wudja were real . . .

Since this could be interesting, I decided not to bitch too much. Just enough to make Mom think things were normal.

"You're leaving me at Cookie's in the middle of the night, and going to Dalton for you don't know how long? And after tonight, I've got to find my own accommodations?"

Without removing his eyes from the road, Roger took Mom's left hand and placed it on her pile of money. He cleared his throat in what sounded like a signal.

Mom said to me, "Well, it's not like I'm leaving you with nothing."

Roger popped the overhead light on again so that Mom could see the cash in her lap. She hesitated, then peeled three hundred-dollar bills off the stack and passed them back to me.

"Don't spend it all in one place. And don't you dare buy drugs, or I'll slap you into the next state!"

I stared at the money. I'd never held a hundred-dollar bill before, let alone three of them.

"So I'm supposed to bribe some kid I used to know to let me crash on her couch?" I asked.

As Mom whirled around in her seat, Roger clicked off the light. He didn't want to see what was coming anymore than I did.

"You hated Tampa!" Mom exclaimed. "Now we're back where you went to school till a month ago! Can't you find one person who'd be happy to see you?"

I wish I could, I thought. Andrew's smile floated in my mind next to a dark hole of fear. I had escaped from Tampa, all right, but the only good reason for being here was gone.

"Tell Easter how to get in touch with you," Roger reminded Mom.

She suddenly sounded exhausted. "When we drop you off at Cookie's, Roger will give you his cell phone number. I have Cookie's number, so I'll leave a message with her saying when I'll be back."

"But I won't be at Cookie's by then," I pointed out.

Mom hates logic because she rarely has any. I could feel the heat of her frustration rolling my way. Roger intervened, sounding as cheerful as the guy who predicts the weather on TV.

"Easter, just check in with Cookie every morning to see if there's a message. And feel free to call me on my cell anytime."

Roger didn't know that Cookie rarely got up before two in the afternoon. Or that it wouldn't be easy for me to call anyone since I didn't have a cell phone. There was no point mentioning either problem. At least I'd have his number.

Plus, I had bigger worries beginning with the fact that Mom seemed to have plans, and I didn't know what they were. What was she up to in Dalton? I couldn't picture her helping a family in need. On a good day, she couldn't even help herself. After Roger's daddy died, then what? Would Roger stay in Dalton, while Mom came back to Atlanta alone? Where would we go from here?

And my biggest worry of all: What if Mom didn't come back for me?

Considering what she does for a living, I didn't expect Cookie to be home from work yet. But she opened the door herself, a cigarette, as usual, dangling from her lips.

"Hey, kid, good to see ya!" She squinted at me through a haze of smoke. "Come on in. Where's Nikki?"

I explained that my mom and her friend had to take off in a hurry on account of Roger's dad being on the verge of death. In fact, Roger had gotten a call from his sister just as we arrived at our old apartment building. She told him their father was asking for him, which probably meant the end was near. Being a gentleman, Roger wanted to see me safely inside, but Mom assured him I would be all right. She said they'd better put the pedal to the metal if he wanted to hear his dad's last words. So Roger gave me his cell number, as promised, and they took off for Dalton.

"Is your sister's family here?" I asked Cookie. If so, they had to be sleeping because the only sound was the TV. Cookie's apartment was exactly like the one we'd lived in for eleven months, but messier. Every available surface was covered with ashtrays and empties—empty bottles, empty cigarette packs, empty cereal boxes, etc. The place smelled like cigarette butts, and a bluish smog hung in the air.

Cookie said, "Tonight's my night off and I just wanted to chill. They all went to a late movie."

She ground out one cigarette and picked up another that was already lit. Cookie always smoked that way, lighting a fresh cigarette before she was quite finished with the old one. I noticed a sleeping bag open on the couch and another spread on the floor.

"It's cozy," Cookie remarked, following my gaze. "My sister and her baby share my room, and her two boys sleep out here."

Cookie must have known what I was thinking because she added, "Don't worry, hon. I'll put down some blankets for you over there."

She waved toward the corner of the living room, which was piled high with toys. Then, without asking, she brought me a Coke and a bag of chips. She'd probably heard my stomach growl.

Cookie parked herself and her cigarettes in front of the TV. She flipped a few channels and said, "Enjoy the quiet while you can. They'll be back any minute. And those kids hate to go to bed."

I thanked Cookie for letting me crash at her place. She said she was sorry she couldn't let me stay longer.

"You got someplace else you can go?" she asked. I assured her I did even though I had no clue where. We watched TV for a while without talking.

Finally, trying to sound casual, I said, "Do you happen to know who moved into our apartment?"

"There's an old guy in there now," Cookie replied. "He's blind, and they put him on the *second* floor. Can you believe it?"

I was trying not to.

"He must have a bird," Cookie added, taking a deep drag on one of the two cigarettes currently burning. "The first few weeks, I heard these god-awful sounds—like a chicken on a chopping block. I haven't heard 'em lately, though, or seen the old guy. Maybe he's moved out already."

I thought about my dream, in which the apartment was empty except for Wudja, who flew out the window.

Cookie continued, "How he got away with having a bird, I'll never know. This place don't allow pets."

They probably don't allow astral-projection, either. And yet it happens . . .

chapter thirteen
UPSTAIRS

When Cookie's phone rang, I guessed it wasn't good news. Even if you work nights, you probably don't get casual calls at two in the morning. Cookie's sister was phoning to say that Cookie's car, which the sister had borrowed, had a flat tire, and there was no spare in Cookie's trunk. Fortunately, Cookie knew exactly where she could borrow another car at that hour. I had a hard time following her half of the conversation, but I gathered that the second car belonged to a guy who lived down the street and owed Cookie "big time." She hung up the phone, stubbed out both cigarettes and said, "Easter, hon, I gotta go. You'll be alright, right?"

As soon as she left, I did three things. First, I opened the windows to let the smoke out. Second, I turned off the TV. And third, I sat very still listening for bird sounds, or any sounds at all, coming from the upstairs apartment. I heard nothing.

I opened my backpack and pawed through it for the one now-worthless thing I'd saved from every place we'd ever lived: the spare key. Even in the depths of my bag, I knew the keychain when my hand closed on it. It was the shape and size of a baby's heart, which, if squeezed hard enough, actually started to beat. Those keys might not open anything ever again, but they were proof that I'd lived somewhere long enough to own a piece of it.

You're supposed to change the lock whenever you move in to a new place. Mom never did, though. She said most people don't do what they're "supposed to," only what they "have to," and usually not even that. Knowing how cheap and lazy our Atlanta landlord was, I figured he hadn't changed the lock after we left. Mr. F didn't follow any rules, so he probably hadn't changed it, either.

Since Cookie hadn't given me a key to her apartment, I was careful to leave it unlocked when I headed upstairs. The building was deathly quiet, more quiet than I ever remembered it from when we lived here. Every detail about the place seemed suddenly magnified: the smell of cooked cabbage seeping from the Kropniks' apartment; the burned-out bulbs in the musty hallway; the echo of my steps on the metal stairs. I paused outside number nine, our old apartment. As in both my dream and my memories, the door was still dented from someone's long-ago kick. There was total silence.

I squeezed the keychain in the palm of my hand, letting the heartbeat give me courage. Cookie said the old man hadn't been around lately. It was the middle of the night, so I wasn't about to pound on his door. All I wanted was to see if I could still enter the apartment the "normal" way. I took a deep breath and slid my spare key into the lock.

Instead of turning, the key became hot in my hand. Not hot in a burning way, but hot in a *live* way. Holding that key was like connecting to another living soul.

And then the familiar transition began—the smell of cooked cabbage grew stronger as the floor tipped me forward into another world.

But it wasn't the world I'd learned to expect. I didn't find myself on the other side of the apartment door facing our old couch in its new position. Instead, I was standing in what looked like a long, dark alley after a rainstorm. The smell of cooked cabbage morphed into the stench from a nearby dumpster. Puddles on the pavement reflected what few lights there were, bare bulbs burning above unmarked metal doors. The night air hung heavy with heat and humidity. Far off was the buzz of steady traffic, possibly on the interstate. I listened closely and heard something else: a distant male voice. Then I noticed that one of the metal doors down the alley was ajar, pale yellow light leaking out. I moved toward it, trying with every step to understand what the voice was saying. It belonged to a young guy, full of passion and purpose. I caught something about "protecting true talent." When I was almost within reach of the door, I realized that he was speaking French.

"I know the procedure," he said with a trace of impatience. "You'll make sure his parents understand and agree. Then they'll stop worrying."

Suddenly there was a second voice, a woman, also speaking French.

"They'll stop worrying when they realize that this is the best way. Our methods are unorthodox, but we offer so much."

I stopped breathing. The woman's voice was familiar. It couldn't be—

When I pulled open the heavy door, its hinges screeched. The two people standing inside spun around to face me. I didn't know the boy, who was dark and slight of build but probably about my age. I did know the woman, although her presence here—where?—made no sense.

"Mme Papinchak," I gasped.

chapter fourteen

RE-STARTERS

"Bienvenue." Mme Papinchak welcomed me in French. She didn't look surprised to see me although I was totally stunned to see her. Like most teachers, she didn't really exist for me outside her classroom. And now, here we were, outside my whole regular life. She whispered something I couldn't hear to the boy who was with her. He gave me an uneasy look and disappeared into the dark recesses of the place, his footsteps echoing long after he was gone. I had the impression we were in a vast warehouse, but the only light was near the door I'd come through.

Mme Papinchak motioned for me to step all the way inside. "You found us, finally," she said in English.

"Found who?" I demanded. "Where are we?"

When she pressed her finger to her lips, I realized that my excited voice was bouncing off walls I couldn't see. Quietly I said, "What are *you* doing here? What am *I* doing here?"

"Before I can answer that, Easter, you'll have to see a little more. Follow me."

Only then did I notice how oddly she was dressed. My French teacher was wearing work boots and coveralls the color of night. Her glasses were gone. And her hair, usually worn loose to her shoulders, was tucked under a dark cap, the visor pulled low over her eyes.

"Watch your step," she said, removing a flashlight from one of her pockets and clicking it on. "We don't use electricity when we can avoid it."

Who's we? I wondered, staying close behind her as she moved into the blackness. We threaded our way through a maze of stacked boxes that rose around us like immense walls. As the flashlight beam swung from side to side, I glimpsed labels for toilet paper, breakfast cereals, and diapers. Muffled voices reached us from somewhere out of sight.

At last we stepped around a corner into a pool of feeble light. A single bare bulb hung from the ceiling barely illuminating two Army cots, a card table, and a couple folding chairs. In one chair sat the boy I'd seen with Mme Papinchak. Across from him was Andrew.

I shrieked with delight and ran to him, but the first boy leaped from his seat and blocked me with both arms.

"Non, non!" cried Mme Papinchak. I didn't know whether she meant me or him until she added, *"Ça, c'est d'accord, Marco."*

"You're Marco?" I echoed.

"That's right," said Andrew. "Easter, meet Marco. He's a little hyped about protecting me."

"I'm so glad you're all right!" I exclaimed and then added quietly, "Is Marco on our side?"

Andrew said, "Marco's the reason I'm here."

I hugged my good friend, burying my face in his feathery, citrus-scented hair. Tears of relief spilled down my cheeks. Everything felt normal except the way Andrew winced when I held him.

"You okay?" I asked.

"Just glad you finally got here."

"You were expecting me?"

"Oh, yes," Andrew replied. "Madame said your astral-projecting was running a little behind schedule."

Confused, I wiped my streaming nose with the back of my hand, then glanced from Andrew to Mme Papinchak. "How can you two know each other?"

"My life's a lot larger than my day job," she said.

Madame promised that Andrew would start the explanations, and then she'd take over. First, though, she insisted I eat something.

"Do you like Mexican?" Marco asked me.

"You speak perfect English!" I gasped.

Andrew laughed. "You thought he didn't?"

"I didn't know. He and Madame were speaking French."

"Marco's Québécois," Mme Papinchak explained. "From Montréal. I like to practice my French when I'm with him."

"I speak Spanish and Italian, too. And English," Marco said. "We used to live in Europe. My dad was in the diplomatic corps. After he died, we moved back to Canada until—"

Madame interrupted to say that she and Marco would go get our food. As soon as they were gone, I asked Andrew what was going on with Marco.

"I sensed from the moment I met him there was something powerful going on. Something beyond my attraction to him. Turns out he was assigned to my case at Homefree."

"Homefree?" My brain whirred. Where had I heard that before? Then I recalled the dream I'd had during the ride up from Tampa. In it, I'd read part of a news story about Andrew that mentioned Homefree, but the story was continued on a page I couldn't find.

Andrew explained, "Homefree is an underground network that moves specially gifted teens out of dangerous situations into safer ones. Along the way are 'substations' like this one—temporary stops before permanent relocation. Marco's a Homefree guide. He used to be a re-starter."

"Re-starter?" I was having trouble keeping up.

"A re-starter is a teen in serious trouble, someone who needs to escape one place and begin again somewhere else."

"Sounds like me," I murmured.

"It is you," Andrew said. "You and me, we're both re-starters."

I stared. "Do you astral-project, too?"

"No. We all have different gifts."

I thought about what Andrew's mother told me in her email and said, "You're here because you're a post-cognitive reader. Right?"

His eyes widened. "You noticed? I wanted to tell you, but I wasn't ready."

"I wasn't ready to tell you about astral-projecting, either." I told Andrew his parents had contacted me. "Your mom's afraid your 'gift' got you in trouble. I started thinking maybe Marco was bad."

Andrew shook his head. "*'Au contraire,'* as Madame would say. Marco's one of the good guys. Wait till you hear about his talent."

"I wouldn't call astral-projecting a 'talent,'" I muttered. "Talents are things like being able to sing or paint. You control your talents, they don't control you. Astral-projecting *happens* to me. I have no control, just like I have no control over the rest of my life."

"That's because you haven't mastered it yet," Andrew said. "I feel the same way about post-cognition. It's hard enough being gay—let alone being able to read people's past experiences just by talking with them."

I realized that Andrew's talent might actually be harder to deal with than my own, and I told him so.

He shrugged. "I don't know. But Marco's gift might be the most useful. He's gay, smart, and way small for his age. When guys started beating him up, he discovered he could *remote-defend.*"

"What's that?"

"Throw punches by using his mind. He saved my ass."

That's when I noticed Andrew's left eye. Our circle of light was dim, but his eye looked shadowed and swollen.

"You got beat up," I said.

"You should see my back. If 'bruise' is a color, I've got every shade of it. That's why Marco didn't want you to touch me."

"Do you still hurt?"

"Not enough to miss your hugs," Andrew said.

"What happened?"

"A couple guys were looking for me—neo-Nazi jerks who hang around my neighborhood. I didn't go to school all week, but they found me. On Thursday I was coming out of the mall, and there they were. I had nowhere to run. They threw me against a wall and started kicking me so hard I thought they'd bust my kidneys. If Marco hadn't been there, I might have died."

"Marco saved you?" I tried to imagine that fine-boned boy using his special talent to fend off two monsters.

"He freaked them out. Charged straight at 'em, screaming every language he knows and waving his arms around. The skinheads thought he was insane. There's nothing more alarming than a fast little guy who's crazy! Except maybe a fast little guy who can throw energy." The memory made Andrew smile. "From six feet away Marco sent them sprawling. They backed off fast, calling us 'freaking faggots.' Then Marco brought me here. I'm waiting while Homefree works out my relocation."

"This is like a warehouse," I said, squinting at the walls of boxes.

Andrew said, "That's exactly what it is. People work here. I hear them moving stuff around all day, but nobody ever comes back to my corner. I don't see anyone till Marco or one of the other guides comes around at night to bring me my dinner."

"How can you stand it?" I asked.

"It's only temporary. Then the rest of my life will begin."

"But what about your parents? They're worried sick about you!"

Andrew looked away. "I hate that part, I really do. But Madame will let them know I'm okay and get their permission to move me to a different city. We'll see each other soon."

A terrifying thought struck me. "Will I have to stay here till my mom gives her okay? Madame might never find her! I could be stuck in this warehouse for the rest of my life!"

Andrew laughed. "Relax. Your deal is totally different. Mme Papinchak will explain."

chapter fifteen

POSSIBLE

Over greasy tacos and enchiladas, which tasted better than anything I'd eaten in years, Mme Papinchak started talking about me and my weird life.

"You have a facility for French. Do you know that, Easter?"

"A facility?" I echoed.

"A natural gift," she said.

"I don't think so. French just isn't that hard."

Andrew snorted. "It's my worst class. I get As in almost everything, and Cs in French."

Madame said, "It doesn't seem hard to you, Easter, because you have an aptitude for it. I saw that your first day at Fowler. And that wasn't all I saw."

"Hard to miss the emerald nose stud, isn't it?" teased Andrew. "Or the hair color. Most girls don't go for that 'asphalt' look."

I threw a straw at him, and he ducked.

"What I saw," Mme Papinchak said, steering the conversation, "was that you were capable of super-corporeal travel."

"Huh?"

"Out-of-body transmissions." When I continued to stare, she added, "Astral-projections. You can zap yourself anywhere."

"No way!" I protested. "I have no control over that stuff! It never even happened to me till I moved to Tampa."

"Are you sure?" Madame gave me a mischievous smile.

"Of course, I'm sure!"

But suddenly, I wasn't. Suddenly, I remembered a strange dream I used to have when I was a kid, probably starting about age five. I would find myself in a place that seemed familiar, and I would see someone I knew doing something dangerous, something that was bound to injure him or her. When I tried to warn the person, I would discover that no one could see or hear me.

For example, I had this dream when I was nine years old. It was so vivid that I could still replay every single second. A girl who lived a few doors down was skipping rope in the middle of the street, and I knew—I just knew—that she was going to get hit by a car if she didn't move. I could hear tires squealing as a vehicle rounded the corner. So I tried to save her. I ran forward to pull her out of the way, screaming until my ears rang.

The dream ended before I saw what happened. As always, I woke up not knowing the outcome. But in real life my friends stayed safe, and every time I had a dream like that, I wondered for a moment if I'd really been asleep.

"You're remembering something, aren't you?" asked Mme Papinchak.

"Just a dream," I mumbled.

"Astral-projections often seem like dreams, especially to the young."

"How would you know?" I demanded.

For a very long moment, Madame just smiled.

I gaped. "You don't mean that you—"

"Yes. I travel out of body, too. In fact . . . that's how I got here tonight."

A chill shot from the top of my head to the soles of my feet.

"But we—we can see you!" I stammered. "We can touch you!"

I had felt Madame brush against me when she and Marco arrived with the food.

"And you're *eating!"* I added. "If you're astral-projecting, you can't do that! It's impossible."

"Really?" I'd never seen such a broad grin on Mme Papinchak's face. "Then how are *you* managing it?"

By then I was trembling so hard I had to clutch the edge of the table just to keep myself in my seat. Madame laid her warm hand on top of mine.

"You don't know what's possible, Easter. But you're about to find out."

chapter sixteen
CONSULTANT

Before I could reply, the room tipped forward at the same time that it started to spin. It was my standard "super-corporeal" experience except for one thing—I could feel Mme Papinchak still holding my hand. Then came the smell of cooked cabbage, and the next thing I knew, we were both in apartment nine, sitting on the couch. I was in the middle, sandwiched between Mr. Fairless on my left and Madame on my right.

"Finally!" the old man croaked. I hadn't heard his voice in a while, so its raspy edge jarred me. "Took you long enough!"

I assumed he was talking to me. To my astonishment, Mme Papinchak replied, "Sorry, Sir. We're running about an hour behind schedule. Slight miscalculation."

"Forgot to factor in her mother's business at the diner, didn't you?" he said.

"Yes, Sir."

Mr. F made a "tsking" sound. "Math never was your strong suit, Jennifer. You should know that by now, and plan accordingly."

"Sorry, Sir. It won't happen again." Mme Papinchak—a.k.a. Jennifer—sounded as contrite as a freshman during the first week of school.

"What about you, Easter?" Mr. F cranked his voice up about a hundred more decibels. Never mind that I was sitting right next to him.

"What about me?"

"Any questions so far?"

Only about a thousand. I wanted to roll my eyes but restrained myself out of respect for Madame, who was having a hard enough time already.

"Uh—where's Wudja?" I asked innocently.

The bird was nowhere to be seen, and the window was closed, just like in my dream. Although I disliked Mr. F's bird, I hoped he hadn't really smashed himself against the glass. I was beginning to doubt whether any of my dreams were just dreams.

"Wudja want a way in! No way! No way!"

I craned my neck toward the familiar squawk. The parrot, looking considerably worse for wear, swayed from his perch on the top of the open closet door. He seemed to have lost about half his feathers, and his remaining plumage stood out at odd angles.

"Guess where he just came from!" demanded Mr. Fairless.

"I'd rather not, Sir," answered Mme Papinchak.

"I'm not talking to *you!"* he snapped. "This is Easter's business."

"Umm . . . I don't know," I murmured.

"You should know!" the bird sang out.

"Most recently, Wudja was in the apartment downstairs," Mr. F said. "Being chased from corner to corner by two hyperactive boys and two screaming women. They returned from a middle-of-the-night emergency to find their windows wide open, *you* missing, and a large bird pooping everywhere! Can you explain any of that?"

I'd rather not, I thought, squeezing my eyes shut.

"So how did Wudja get back home?" I asked.

"Funny you should ask," began Mr. F. "A lady with the name of a dessert and the breath of a dragon knocked on my door. It was three in the morning. After I listened to her story, I opened my window, called Wudja, and he flew one flight up." Mr. F cleared his throat. "I have some advice for you, Easter. Don't mess with other people's windows."

I wanted to protest that I had messed with his window *in my dream*, but I said nothing.

Mr. F added, "You need to let Dragon-Breath-Dessert Lady know you're all right. It's irresponsible to teleport without reassuring your host."

"Teleport?"

"Total body projection to a secondary locale," supplied Mme Papinchak. "In other words, what you just did."

I looked at Mr. F. "I'm supposed to tell people when I 'teleport'?"

"Of course not!" he said. "You're supposed to tell people when you leave. It's common courtesy."

"What should I say to Cookie?"

"Tell her you're with me." Mme Papinchak sounded inspired. From one of her coverall pockets, she produced a tasteful business card, which read "Jennifer C. Papinchak, Consultant," followed by an Atlanta address and phone number.

"Consultant?" I asked. "What do you consult about?"

"Whatever needs explaining."

So far, she hadn't explained a thing.

"You live in Atlanta, but you teach in Tampa?" I asked, looking at her card.

"Sometimes." Madame gave me a look that said we were sticking to her agenda. "I suggest you write a note to

Cookie and enclose my card. Tell her to call me when she wants to talk to you. Leave the note under her door, and let's go."

"Where?"

Mr. F chose that moment to clear his throat, a disgusting procedure that reminded me of starting a lawn mower. At last, he coughed, spat, and pronounced, "Enough questions! You have a job to do."

"Get to work!" cawed Wudja, who flapped furiously from atop the open closet door.

Mme Papinchak handed me a box of stationery and a pen. Did those come from her pockets, too?

Quickly I wrote the note, enclosed Madame's card, and addressed the envelope to Cookie. Then I hesitated.

"Should I walk downstairs—or . . . you know?"

"Astral-projection is not a labor-saving device!" Mr. F roared. Then he turned to Mme Papinchak and said, "You've got your work cut out for you with this one."

"Yes, Sir," she said, sounding weary already.

So I walked downstairs and slid the note under Cookie's door. There was no point knocking. Why disturb the kids sleeping in the living room? Cookie would find the note soon enough, or her nephews would. In any case, Cookie now had a way to reach me when Mom called to say she was coming back. If Mom called.

The sky outside Mr. F's window was graying toward a new day when I returned from my delivery.

"Where did—?" I began, but Madame shushed me. The old man and his parrot were gone.

"They need their rest," she whispered. "And we need to get to work. How are you feeling?"

"Confused," I said.

"Ça c'est bon," she replied. "People learn best when most uncertain."

Madame explained that she would be shadowing me for a while, staying out of sight unless I needed her.

"How will you know if I need you?" I asked.

"I'll know."

That wasn't much comfort when I had so many questions. "Where am I going? What am I supposed to do?"

"You'll figure it out," she said, checking her watch.

So far, Madame's consulting skills sucked. Plus, she was getting impatient.

I tried again. "Will I be invisible, like I was before, or will I—what do you call it—'teleport'?"

Madame said, *"N'importe. Allons-y!"*

Maybe it didn't matter to her, but I would have liked to know. Too late. The room was already spinning, and I distinctly tasted fresh pineapple. *Au revoir*, Atlanta.

chapter seventeen
BUSINESS

I knew who was talking before the room came into focus. Short Ron McWithy, the man who was my stepfather for less than a year, has a voice you couldn't forget if you wanted to. It's sharp and high for a man, plus Short Ron talks super-fast. Then again, Short Ron is a little guy who moves fast. Not a freak of nature exactly, but no taller than five foot five, with his boots on. And Short Ron never stands still.

Before their marriage fell apart, Mom would say that Short Ron was "excitable." Later she called him "jumping-jack crazy" because he hopped and waved when he was wrought up. Mom married Short Ron thinking he was eccentric on the way to wealthy. Turned out he was just plain nuts.

Short Ron was "jumping-jack crazy" when I arrived from Atlanta via the Super-Corporeal Express.

"Of course, I'm cutting corners!" he shouted. "How else am I gonna make money? How else are *you* gonna have a job? Answer me that, Mr. Genius!"

"But what you're doing, it ain't right."

The second voice, softer and deeper, was familiar, too. I recognized it instantly, and then my vision cleared. Even slouching, Cal Wacker towered over Short Ron. At first I couldn't tell where we were. Then I realized that this was Short Ron's old office for his doomed used-car dealership back when he and Mom were married. Now it looked like a computer workshop. Half-assembled—or half-unassembled—units covered the counters, and boxes of what I assumed were computer components lined the walls.

I checked myself—very wavy. Based on past experience, that meant I was invisible. I looked around for Mme Papinchak but saw no sign that she had traveled with me. So much for counting on her services.

Short Ron was waving his small hands around as he talked. "You may be a whiz with computers, Cal, but you don't know a darn thing about business. The whole point is to make a profit! And you make a profit by giving folks what they want for less money than they'd have to pay the guy down the street. Now, how are ya gonna do that?"

"By reducing overhead," Cal mumbled. The way he said it, I could tell Short Ron had force-fed him the line.

"Exactly right! And how you gonna reduce overhead in a business with profit margins as narrow as this one?"

When Cal didn't answer right away, Short Ron did a little jump. "Come on, boy, what did I teach you?"

"Well . . ." Cal shifted his weight from one size thirteen foot to the other. "You taught me to look for ways to cut corners . . ."

"Which is what I done! Now what's your problem with that?"

Cal pulled himself up to his full height, which was about six foot two.

"My problem, sir, is that we tell people we rebuild computers with genuine Intel processors, but we're using bootleg chips from Taiwan."

"So what?" Short Ron crossed his arms over his chest and glared up at Cal. "You think Joe Lunchbox can tell the difference?"

"No, but the next guy he takes his computer to surely can."

"*We're* the next guy he takes his computer to!" Short Ron said.

"But what if we're not?"

"Use your head, boy! It's all part of the plan!"

Short Ron jumped excitedly around the room as he talked. The space was so cramped that I had to scramble to stay out of his way.

"We build 'em, they break. We fix 'em, they break again. Then we fix 'em again! And again! The money keeps rolling in. I tell you, it's beautiful!"

Cal looked worried. "My daddy always said you need a good reputation if you're gonna stay in business."

"Well, your daddy never had a pot to piss in, did he? God rest his soul. Nice guy but clueless about business. I wouldn't follow his advice if I was you."

"The thing is, sir, that a lot of folks in this town weren't happy with the cars you sold them back when this was a dealership."

Short Ron waved that worry away. "Pissants and crybabies. I don't do business with them types no more. We got us a high-class clientele now. We ain't selling used cars here, boy. These are intellectual tools."

A bell sounded from the next room, indicating a possible customer.

"Be right with ya!" Cal called.

"And remember what I said about keeping a smile on your face," Short Ron said. "Ya gotta give the buying public a happy sales experience."

Cal nodded and shuffled out to the lobby. Short Ron plopped down in a tattered plaid recliner that was stuck in extended position. He stretched himself out for a nap.

"I understand that you sell rebuilt computers here," came a woman's voice from the sales room. Not just any woman; it was the voice of Mme Papinchak.

"Yes, ma'am, that's right, we do," Cal replied. "How can I help you today?"

"Your sign out front says that you use only genuine Intel parts, but your prices are so low. What kind of guarantee do you offer?"

Cal cleared his throat like there were feathers stuck in there. "We offer a thirty-day warranty, ma'am."

"Only thirty days? For Intel Pentium?"

By then I was peeking around the corner at Madame. She had changed out of her Homefree cap and coveralls into a floral skirt and a white cotton shirt, the kind of outfit she wore at Fowler High. Her reddish brown hair hung straight to her shoulders, and her black-framed glasses were back in place. Still, it stunned me to see her in Short Ron's store.

Cal cleared his throat again. I could tell he was having a moral crisis.

"Well, the thing is, see, that's how we keep our costs so low."

"I don't understand," Madame said. "Doesn't Intel stand behind their products? They should reimburse *you*, the vendor, if anything you sell fails and you have to replace it."

"You'd think so, wouldn't you," Cal murmured. "Uh—could you excuse me for a second? I think I left a soldering iron burning back there . . ."

When Cal darted past me, I glanced at Madame, and we made eye contact. That was unnerving because my still-wavy self told me I was invisible. Then again, Madame and I were operating on a different level. She winked, which I assumed meant that everything was all right even though I had no idea what we were up to.

In the back room, Cal was waking Short Ron from his nap.

"I'm sorry, but I can't do this no more," Cal whispered.

"Say what?" Short Ron sat up, blinking.

"You got a real smart customer out there, and I can't lie to her. I quit."

"You can't quit, dumb ass! How you gonna make a living in this town?"

"I'll find a way. Good luck, Short Ron."

"Wait! What about my daughter? No way you can support Ronni by flipping burgers! My little girl likes to live in style!"

But Cal was already gathering up his tools.

"That's between me and Ronni," he said.

Short Ron scrambled to his feet.

"You can't leave me in the lurch like this! I'll tell everybody I know you're a quitter!"

"Better a quitter than a thief," Cal said, zipping his tool bag closed.

"You watch your mouth, boy!"

Suddenly the stench of scorched metal stung my nostrils. I glanced at the workbench behind Short Ron in time to see a soldering iron flare blood red. Short Ron smelled it, too. He whirled around, saw the super-hot tool and gasped, "Whoa, Nelly! Are you trying to burn this place down?!"

When he yanked the electrical plug from the wall, a spray of sparks arced toward him. Short Ron yelped and jumped back.

I peered out at Madame in the lobby. She made a gesture I couldn't quite grasp. When she repeated it, I understood. But I didn't want to believe it was possible. She was signaling me to follow Cal Wacker, my former boyfriend, and make myself visible to him.

Cal headed out the back door, Short Ron shouting after him: "You're a loser just like your old man!"

"My old man was a winner in every way that mattered," Cal said. And he was gone.

Short Ron took a beat to pump himself up like a rooster at a cock fight. Then he swaggered out to the sales room.

"Morning, ma'am. I'm Short Ron McWithy, owner of this fine establishment. And I'm here to offer you the personal touch in complete computer service."

chapter eighteen
INVISIBLE

As soon as Short Ron stepped into the sales room, I opened the back door and looked around for Cal. He was about ten feet away, tossing his tool bag into the back seat of that sweet cherry-red car with the big fins.

Even though I'd never done anything like it before, I knew that making myself visible to my seventh-grade boyfriend would take a little planning. I mean, I couldn't just materialize in his face. So, still invisible, I slipped into the back seat a second before he slammed the door. Wherever Cal Wacker was going, I was along for the ride. And I needed to think.

What would I say? How could I explain turning up in West Virginia with no suitcase? I didn't even have a purse.

Merci, Mme Papinchak, I thought. You pushed me into action, but I have no idea what kind of action I'm supposed to take.

Cal blasted his radio at full volume, drumming his fingers on the steering wheel as he drove. Within a few minutes, I knew where we were headed: to the McWithy house. Cal was going to tell Ronni what he'd done. This wouldn't be pretty, but apparently Madame wanted me to see it.

I slid over the front seat just as Cal was unfolding his frame from the car. Being small and quick has its advantages—I got out before Cal had time to turn around. For just a second we were so close that I could smell his sweat. It was muskier now than when he was thirteen, and I liked it.

The McWithys' back door was unlocked, just the way it always was when I lived there. I stepped in directly behind Cal. He called, "Ronni! Come on down here! We need to talk!"

When she didn't answer, Cal bounded up the staircase, taking two or three steps at a time. I couldn't keep up, but his voice drifted back to me.

"Ronni! You awake?"

He pounded on her bedroom door.

From the other side, Ronni said, "Are you trying to give me a heart attack in my sleep?"

I reached the landing just as Cal pushed open Ronni's door and barged in. She gave a mock scream.

"Can't a girl have her privacy? I might be naked in here!"

"I hope you are," Cal said.

Ronni, who wasn't naked, sat up in bed. "Aren't you supposed to be at work?"

"I was at work. Now I'm here. I want you to hear this from me and not your old man." Cal sat down on the edge of her bed. "I'm sorry, hon, but I had to quit."

Ronni's eyes bulged. The soft, sleepy expression she'd worn a minute earlier morphed into a look of pure horror.

"What do you mean, you *quit?* That job was our future!"

Cal shook his head. "I hate to tell you this, but I got to: Your daddy's cheating his customers, and I can't be part of it."

"What do you mean, 'cheating his customers'?" Ronni's nasal voice was cold.

Cal explained about the counterfeit chips.

Ronni said, "What's wrong with that?"

"Just about everything! Can't you see?"

Ronni yawned and stretched. Then she motioned for Cal to get up off her bed, and she swung her shapely legs over the side.

"Listen here," she said, glaring up at him. "There's cheating, and then there's *cheating*. One's a sin, cuz you do it to be mean, and the other's what you got to do to stay in business. Don't tell me you're too dumb to know the difference!"

"Cheating is cheating, Ronni. What your daddy's doing ain't right."

Ronni crossed the room to the open closet and started rifling through tousled racks of clothes. I could see how torn up Cal was as he watched her. Ronni's one of those petite types—tiny but curvy. Every guy loves that look, and Cal knew he was about to kiss it goodbye.

"My daddy's a business genius," Ronni said, pulling a sundress over her head and then peeling her night shirt off from underneath. "He was willing to teach you everything he knows."

"Oh, come on! Short Ron's lost every business he's had," Cal said. "First the vacuum cleaner sales, then the used cars. You of all people ought to know that."

Ronni tossed her head and stepped in front of the mirror. I almost leaped out of my skin, for there was my wavy reflection right next to hers. But she didn't react, and neither did Cal, who was watching her in the glass. Then I remembered my projection to the bathroom in Muncie, Indiana. The big blonde hadn't seen me in that mirror, either.

Ronni said, "My daddy was going to let you live here for free. Now where will you go? When your aunt gets married and moves to Cleveland next month, you'll be homeless. And jobless, I might add."

She was right. Cal's mom had died from complications following childbirth, and his dad raised him till Cal was eleven or twelve. Mr. Wacker drove a cab, and one night he got killed by a drunk driver. After that Cal went to live with his only other relative, an aunt.

"I'll be fine," Cal said, but I could tell he was forcing the optimism.

"Plus, you'll have to give up that car. My daddy got you a sweet deal on the payments. But he won't be helping you no more."

"I'll figure out how to keep the car," said Cal. "There are lots of ways to make money."

"Yeah, and they all involve cheating somebody. Wake up and smell the coffee!"

Rocco chose that moment to sink his claws into the back of my neck. He must have been watching from a shelf on the bookcase behind me, but I didn't notice him until he used me as a human step.

I heard myself scream, and in my wavy reflection I saw my mouth open wide. Nobody but Rocco reacted. The cat meowed irritably as he bounced from my shoulders to the floor. I wiped my neck with my hand. Blood.

"Get that disgusting critter out of here," Ronni barked. "He tracks in every kind of dirt. Fur and feathers, too. Whatever he just ate."

Cal didn't move.

"Did you hear me?" Ronni asked. "I told you, get him out of here." She was brushing her spiky hair.

Cal stood staring at her reflection. Or was it at my reflection? For just an instant, I was sure our eyes met.

"What's the matter with you?" Ronni demanded.

"Something just hit me," Cal said.

"What?"

"Uh—this is hard . . ." He cleared his throat. "Life's full of goodbyes, and we're never ready for them."

He stepped up behind her and wrapped his arms around her waist. I saw Ronni stiffen, but she didn't pull away.

"We were cool together, Ronni. You're so darn cute." Tenderly Cal kissed the spikes of her hair. "I'll never forget you."

Then he spun on his heel and strode from the room.

"You can't quit me!" Ronnie sputtered. She turned and aimed her hairbrush at the back of Cal's head. But before she could fire, the brush flew from her hand straight up to the ceiling and bounced back down, ricocheting off the bed to land at her feet. She swore and scooped it up.

I hurried after Cal, accidentally stepping on Rocco's tail. The cat yowled.

"Oh, shut up!" Ronni said and lobbed her hairbrush at him. It struck my left ankle, but I kept moving.

chapter nineteen
VISIBLE

The back door slammed, and I knew that Cal had left the house. I ran down the stairs, determined to catch up with him before he could drive away even though I had no idea what to do next.

Something happened when I tried to open the back door. I felt a zing of energy, and the cold, total solidness of the metal knob in my hand. Looking down, I saw that I was no longer wavy. I was as fully present in Ronni's kitchen as I had been in the Atlanta warehouse.

Cal was almost to his cherry-red car when I burst onto the porch.

"Hello, Calvin Wacker!" I called.

He glanced up and froze.

"Easter Hutton—is that you?"

"In the flesh," I said, barely able to believe it myself.

I hoped I looked cooler than I felt; Cal's face told me I just might. After a few seconds of shock and confusion, what I saw there was pure appreciation. He started walking toward me, his arms out.

My heart ka-booming, I met him halfway. He hugged me so hard that I couldn't breathe. Then he whooped, lifted me off the ground, and swung me around. That was pure Cal—an enthusiastic blend of muscle and joy. Hugging him was the next best thing to being happy. Or maybe that's what being happy is—finding perfection in a moment and making it your own.

"What the heck are you doing in Wheeling?" he asked, still holding me.

Wasn't that the million-dollar question? I cleared my throat, hoping for either the sudden appearance of Mme Papinchak or a brilliant flash of inspiration. When neither materialized, I said, "I need your help."

Without blinking, Cal said. "Sure. What's up?"

And then I told him. Not about Homefree or the astral-projections, but about the mess in my real life, about my mom being on the lam with a guy not much older than Cal and about me being dumped in Atlanta with nowhere to crash. Cal stood there listening and nodding until I was finished. Finally, he looked up at the McWithy house and asked if I wanted to talk to Ronni or Short Ron.

"No way!" I said. "I came here to find you."

If Cal thought that was peculiar, he didn't let on. He opened the passenger door and told me to climb in.

"It's easier to solve problems on a full stomach," he declared. "How about we go get us some chili dogs at the DQ?"

I agreed. Cal didn't ask how I'd traveled from Georgia to West Virginia or why I didn't have so much as a purse. He probably assumed I'd taken off in a hurry and hitchhiked. Typical Cal. He never was one to waste time on what went before, only on figuring out what to do next.

At the DQ, Cal knew everybody. I remembered a few of the kids, but they just stared. I couldn't blame them. When I used to live there, I had brown hair and no nose stud. Plus, I wasn't happy, so I didn't make many friends.

After Cal bought the food, we settled in a corner booth where everything—the seats, table, floor, and wall—was sticky. Between huge bites, he told me what was going on with Short Ron. I wasn't surprised that Cal was good with computers. Back when I first met him, he loved playing video games and figuring out how all kinds of things worked.

Cal replayed what I'd witnessed at Short Ron's that morning. No omissions, except the flaring soldering iron. The whole time he was talking, I was distracted by two facts: (1) I had no idea what I was supposed to do next, and (2) I was attracted to him.

About distraction number two: I hadn't felt this way toward a guy since leaving Wheeling. And I'd lived in three other places. True, we hadn't stayed long in St. Augustine, we'd barely got settled in Tampa, and in Atlanta I'd hung out with Andrew, who was gay. Still, I was amazed that Cal could make me feel this way after so much time and distance . . . and I couldn't stop wondering if he felt the same about me. Oh, I knew he'd been in love with Ronni, or thought he had, right up to about an hour ago. If he was over her, my timing was awesome. If he was on the rebound, my timing sucked.

"What happened to your neck?" Cal asked, his mouth full of hot dog bun.

"What do you mean?"

"Looks like a cat got ya."

I reached for the spot that Rocco had scratched. "Uh—no. Tree branch. I didn't see it."

"Yeah?" Cal didn't sound so sure. Then he laughed. "Same old Easter. Your mind's always someplace else."

"Not always," I said.

He pried tiny napkins from the metal dispenser on our table and passed half of them to me; the rest he used to wipe his mouth and hands.

"So, I reckon we both got to make our own way," he said finally. "Where do you want to end up?"

My answer was automatic. "Homefree."

"Is that in Georgia?" Cal asked.

"I don't know," I admitted. "Wherever it is, it's better than where we are now."

When Cal leaned forward on his elbows, I knew he was ready to listen.

chapter twenty

YES

Nobody could accuse Cal Wacker of having too much imagination. When I told him about astral-projecting, he looked doubtful. When I described Mr. F and Wudja, he laughed out loud.

"You always did like to fun me," Cal said. "I remember those dreams you said you had."

"What dreams?"

"Oh, you'd save somebody's life, only they didn't know you were there cuz you were invisible."

I took a deep breath and reached for both Cal's hands.

"I'm being totally serious," I said, peering deep into his blue eyes. "I don't know how it works, but I can travel with or without my body. Sometimes I fill it in later, like I did today."

I paused to let him say something, anything, but he didn't, so I went on.

"And those dreams? Turns out they weren't dreams, after all. They were my first astral-projections. I just figured that out."

"So . . . you got like magic powers?" Cal asked. I could tell he was trying to keep his voice neutral.

"No. It's just a talent, like the way you can play basketball and fix computers."

"Lots of guys can do that. What you're talking about, that's a whole lot different." He glanced out the window facing the parking lot, and then back at me. Now his eyes were deeply serious. "Easter, when I was in Ronni's room—well, I saw you . . . in her mirror. I saw Rocco scratch you. And I heard you scream."

"Wow," I whispered, squeezing his hands.

"There's more," he said. "Sometimes, when I get real upset, I . . . *move* things. Do you know what I'm talking about?"

"Like Ronni's hairbrush?" I asked. I decided not to mention seeing the soldering iron flare in Short Ron's workshop.

Cal nodded. "I knew she was gonna throw it at me, so I 'disabled' it. Creepy, huh?"

"Don't ask me how this works," I said, "but we're in it together. Does it scare you? Because it definitely scares me."

Cal shrugged. "Lot of things are scary, but I don't let that worry me. I look at what I can fix or change, and I go from there."

He asked how he fit into my Homefree mission. Before I had to admit that I didn't know, a voice said, "Excuse me. May I join you two?"

Mme Papinchak was standing by our table. Dressed as she had been in Short Ron's shop, she held a steaming cup of coffee and a banana split.

Cal blinked at her in surprise. Then he said, "Why sure," and slid over to make room in our booth.

Madame smiled at me in what I thought was an approving way. Indicating her ice cream, she said, "Traveling makes me hungry."

"You're from out of town?" Cal asked.

"I'm from Homefree," she said.

Cal glanced from Madame to me and back to Madame. "So you two are together?"

"We're part of a team," she said. "How much has Easter explained?"

"Well, she told me about the projections and the old man and the bird—"

I interrupted to add, "Cal saw me in Ronni's mirror!"

"Of course, he did," Madame said briskly. "Cal's what we call a Sensitive, someone who can sense a presence most others are unaware of."

Cal shook his head in wonder. "I'd call myself mighty confused."

Madame laughed, and I was struck by how musical it sounded.

"This doesn't match your expectations, does it? So little of life does. By the way, I'm Jennifer Papinchak. Easter calls me Madame."

She offered Cal her hand. Taking it, he said, "Is it all right if I call you Ma'am?"

"Sure," she said. Then she gave Cal her business card, a different one than she'd given me. This card listed her title not as "Consultant," but as "Placement Specialist." It featured a toll-free number and a P.O. Box in St. Augustine, Florida.

"How does this here Homefree work?" Cal asked, tapping her card.

Madame explained that Homefree was an all-volunteer underground network committed to relocating endangered young people so that they could have a fresh start.

"You reckon I'm *endangered?"* Cal asked.

"Perhaps not physically, although your former boss has a mean streak," Madame said. "My mission within Homefree is to identify and place marginalized teens who have special potential that would otherwise go undeveloped. That's where you fit in."

Cal looked genuinely surprised. "I'm not that special, Ma'am . . ."

"We think you are. Not only are you good with technology, but you also have an integrity rarely seen in sixteen-year-olds. And then there's the PK."

"PK?" Cal repeated.

"Psychokinesis. Your ability to move matter with your mind. Surely you've noticed."

Cal gulped and mumbled, "I've been trying to ignore that . . ."

Madame nodded. "A typical response to powers and events we don't understand. I should add that I believe you have leadership potential."

Cal grinned with pride. "Wish my daddy could hear you say that."

"Easter helped me identify you without even realizing she was doing it. Now I'd like to bring you into our network."

"He doesn't have to live in that warehouse, does he?" I asked with alarm. Cal was an outdoors kind of guy who loved to fish and hunt. I couldn't imagine him penned up in a gloomy big-city warehouse.

"No," Madame said. "Every case is different. We'd like to move Cal directly to Homefree Headquarters."

"Where's that?" he and I said.

"St. Augustine. We have a very good private school there. Homefree participants not only do meaningful work, but they also receive a first-rate education." Madame regarded Cal. "You can join us as soon as your aunt gives her permission. She's your legal guardian, am I right?"

"Yeah, but she's about done with me. Next month, she's marrying a Northern guy who's got three kids and don't want one more."

"We understand," said Madame, "but your aunt needs to sign off on this. I'm prepared to explain to her how we can help you. *If* you want to do this, Cal. It's completely up to you."

He frowned thoughtfully. "I can't say I understand what you're talking about, but what I've heard so far sounds good. And there ain't much to keep me here in Wheeling. Is Easter going to St. Augustine, too?"

Good question, I thought, and wished I'd asked it myself.

"Easter has more fieldwork to do first," Madame replied.

Cal was getting a pretty good deal. Nobody had asked me whether or not I wanted to join Homefree. I was minding my own business when I got zapped to an old blind guy's apartment and found myself with a parrot on my head.

"Is Andrew going to St. Augustine?" I asked Madame.

"We're still negotiating with his parents," she said.

"Who's Andrew?" Cal asked.

"A guy I knew in Atlanta. He's in Homefree, too," I said.

"Is he your boyfriend?"

I was thrilled that Cal cared. "Andrew's got a boyfriend. He's gay."

Cal looked relieved. Madame asked him again whether he wanted to do this. He spread his fingers on the table and studied them.

"Well, I reckon my life ain't going anywhere good if I stay in this town with no family and no job," he said slowly. "I always knew Easter was special, so if she could convince somebody that I'm worth looking at, then . . ."

"Is that a 'yes'?" asked Madame.

"That's a 'yes,' Ma'am."

chapter twenty-one

NO

As soon as she'd finished her coffee, Madame announced that it was time for Cal and me to say goodbye.

"Goodbye?" I echoed. "Can't I go with you?"

Madame said, "You still have fieldwork to do, remember? They're expecting Cal and me at Homefree Headquarters."

"Who's 'they'?" I asked.

Ignoring my question, Madame stood up. Her leather purse made a sound like peeling tape when she removed it from the sticky table. Cal and I rose, too. He put his arm around me.

"When can I see Easter again, Ma'am?"

"That will be up to Mr. Fairless," she replied.

"But we will see each other, right?" I asked. "And Andrew—will I see him? I left the warehouse without saying goodbye."

Behind her glasses, a shadow crossed Madame's eyes. "I'm in no position to promise anything."

Before I could protest, Cal squeezed my shoulders and kissed the top of my head, the way I'd seen him kiss Ronni goodbye.

"It's okay," he whispered. "You just take care till I see you again."

Madame frowned at her wristwatch. "Cal, we need to go."

"What about me?" I asked. "Am I supposed to hang around the DQ in Wheeling till I get zapped someplace else?"

My words came out louder than intended. Kids in the next booth turned and stared. Madame produced one of those adult looks that says, "Get a grip." Then she opened her purse and took out a cell phone.

"You need to talk to Cookie. Your mother left you a message."

Uneasily, I accepted the phone. "Is everything all right?"

"Comme si, comme ça," she replied.

"You speak Spanish?" Cal asked.

Madame said she'd wait outside while Cal and I made our goodbyes.

"What about your phone?" I asked.

"That's your phone," she said. "Whatever you do, don't lose it."

Saying so long to Cal wasn't unbearable after all. He pointed to my new phone and predicted that we'd talk soon even though he didn't have a cell, and I didn't know my own number.

"In this operation, I reckon every question gets answered eventually," he said. Then he kissed me again—on the mouth this time. It almost turned me inside out. Cal had not only grown up since I'd seen him last; he'd also learned how to kiss. Ronni's loss was going to be some lucky girl's gain . . .

As I stood there in the DQ, watching Cal and Madame drive off in his cherry-red car, my new cell phone rang.

"Easter? Is that you?" Instantly I recognized the husky voice.

"Hi, Cookie. What's going on?"

She took a drag on one of her cigarettes and said, "Hon, your mom called me this morning. I wanted to make sure you got the message. She said it looks like Roger's father's going to take a long time to die. Now that his son's there with him, he's perked right up."

"What does that mean?" I asked.

"I don't think Nikki's coming back to Atlanta anytime soon. You doing all right?"

I told her I was fine even though I felt a thousand miles from okay.

"So you're staying with the lady whose card you gave me, right?" Cookie asked.

I lied that I was.

She said "the lady" had called and told Cookie that she could now reach me direct at this number. I asked Cookie to tell me what that number was. Since I didn't have anything to write with, I had to memorize it, which wasn't hard. The last four digits were the month and day I was born. Coincidence? I didn't think so. Cookie promised to give Mom my number the next time she called.

"You left your backpack and another bag in my apartment," Cookie said. "Do you need them?"

That's when I remembered the three hundred bucks Mom had given me. I'd rolled the money up and slipped it into the smallest pocket in my khakis. I felt for it; the cash was still there. Relief washed over me. I told Cookie I'd get my bags later.

"Okay, hon. They'll be here whenever you and your mom come by. "

I wondered when—or if—that would happen.

Cookie was saying goodbye when the DQ started spinning, and her voice gave way to a hum of activity. The odors changed, too. Gone were the aromas of stale coffee, hot dogs, and chili sauce. Now I smelled what could only be a school cafeteria: sour milk, processed cheese, grease, and sweat. It wasn't Saturday anymore.

"Here she comes. Are you ready?"

The voice was familiar—a throaty purr. Then the big blonde from my Muncie, Indiana, bathroom appeared before me. She was huddled at a cafeteria table with the two girls I'd seen last time—small, dark-haired Jolene and tall, athletic Sarah Armbruster, who used to be my neighbor.

"I'm ready," said Jolene. "I can't wait."

Both girls looked at Sarah.

"What about you?" the big blonde demanded.

"I just don't want her to get hurt," Sarah mumbled.

The blonde groaned. "Why should you even care?"

Sarah shrugged. She looked like she'd rather be anywhere else.

"Uh oh, Terra. Sarah's scared," Jolene said, in a taunting voice. "She might get in trouble."

"That's not it," Sarah snapped. "I just don't like scenes, that's all."

"Well, you'd better learn to like them. And fast," the big blonde named Terra declared. "It's how we show the world who's boss. Nobody messes with the Altos."

Jolene said, "I love our name. Sounds like 'The Sopranos'—only scarier. We're the chicks to fear."

"Amber never messed with us," Sarah pointed out.

"Amber made the mistake of thinking she can be one of us if she tries hard enough," said Jolene.

"We let her try, but we keep on punishing her," Terra said. "By making her do what we want. She'll never be cool enough to sit at our table, but she'll never stop trying."

Jolene added, "When we mess her up, we show the other girls at this school that they'd better respect us. Here she comes!"

I followed her gaze to a thin girl with glasses and stringy, shoulder-length hair that was almost colorless. She approached carrying a tray. I counted two beverages and a bowl of soup. This was going to be ugly. A quick check of my wavy self confirmed that no one could see me.

The girl who must be Amber Reston smiled hopefully, but the Altos pretended not to see her. As she drew close to their table, Terra slid her big foot into the aisle. Down Amber went, the tray and its contents suddenly airborne. She groaned when she hit the tile floor, at the same instant that Jolene inverted two single-serving cartons of milk on her head.

"Now!" cried Terra. She was talking to Sarah, who hadn't moved. Sarah was staring at the dripping girl sprawled on the floor.

Terra reached across the table and grabbed a bowl of soup from Sarah's tray. In one fluid motion she flung its contents onto Amber's back. It couldn't have been scalding hot, for the target gave no sign of being burned. In fact, she didn't react. Amber remained on her knees and elbows, her face downcast, as milk streamed over her glasses, and chicken noodle soup soaked her shirt.

Terra grinned with satisfaction and then stood. When she picked up her own fully loaded tray and raised it menacingly over Amber, I could bear no more.

"No!" I cried, lunging toward her. "No, no, *no!*"

chapter twenty-two
ALMOST

Terra groaned and staggered back a step, but she didn't fall or even lose her grip on the tray. And I had hit her with all my might! I was still wavy, though, which meant I wasn't fully there and had only a fraction of my usual strength.

My defensive maneuver wasn't wasted, however. Terra was badly shaken.

"What just happened?" she asked, the items on her tray still shivering.

"I think you slipped in the soup. Or maybe the milk," Jolene said. "Looked like you were going down."

"Yeah," Terra said. "I almost lost my balance."

From the floor came a voice so quiet that it was barely a whisper: "Please stop. Please."

Peering up at them through noodles and milk, Amber looked half-drowned. When Sarah reached down to help her up, Jolene smacked Sarah's arm.

"Let her get up by herself. If she can . . ."

"What's going on over there?"

The new voice belonged to a stocky older woman who was hustling toward the Altos' table. She had gray-brown hair and bushy eyebrows and wore a beige sweater. With the sleeves pushed half-way up her thick arms, she looked ready for a fight. When she spotted Amber Reston on the floor, she gasped and bent over to pull her up.

"She fell down, Mrs. Keppo," Jolene said quickly.

"How on earth—?" said the teacher.

"You know Amber," Terra said. "She's a klutz."

Jolene added, "She tripped over her own big feet and knocked our food off the table. She should watch where she's walking."

"Is that what happened, Amber?" the teacher asked. As the dripping girl stood, a hoot went up from the next table.

"Girl overboard!" a guy shouted, followed by a chorus of laughter.

Somebody else said, "Looks like they pushed her in."

"Amber?" the teacher repeated. "What's going on?"

"Nothing, Mrs. Keppo," Amber mumbled, her voice barely audible, her eyes on the floor. She attempted to shake some liquid from her shirt, which was plastered to her back.

"You're all right?" the teacher asked.

"She's fine," Terra said. "But she's wearing my lunch."

Mrs. Keppo frowned at the big blonde and then at Jolene. When her eyes moved to Sarah Armbruster, they narrowed.

"I'm disappointed to find *you* at this table." With one sweeping glance, she considered the Altos. "I don't want to see anything like this again, is that understood?"

Jolene said, "Then somebody better teach Amber how to walk and chew gum at the same time."

"I'll be more careful," murmured Amber. "Sorry."

Sorry? I couldn't stand it.

"You should be sorry," Terra said. "Thanks to you, I almost fell. Do you know how slippery this floor is?"

"I'll clean it up," Amber offered.

"Oh no you won't," said Mrs. Keppo. "These three will take care of it. You go clean yourself up."

She placed her broad hands on Amber's shoulders and turned her toward the restroom. Like a zombie, Amber shuffled off. Mrs. Keppo glared again at the Altos, her hot eyes lingering on Sarah. "None of you leave until you've cleaned this to my satisfaction. Now get to it!"

"Mr. Gunther's giving a quiz today. It starts in five minutes—" Terra protested.

"That's too bad," Mrs. Keppo said. "The janitor's closet is over there."

I hovered close to Amber as she passed table after table of gawking, laughing kids. One jerk pitched an apple core at her. It narrowly missed my wavy nose and struck Amber's right ear. She didn't flinch.

"I thought it would stick!" the thrower said to an appreciative audience.

"This one will!" A second guy at his table fired off a peeled chunk of banana. It might have lodged in Amber's goopy hair had I not raised my hand to deflect it. The banana bounced back into the first kid's face.

"Hey!" he bellowed and shoved the second kid, who instantly swung back. Mrs. Keppo was hustling toward them as I sailed into the restroom behind Amber.

Without checking herself in the mirror, Amber removed her smudged glasses and washed them methodically under the tap. I studied her reflection: eyes empty, mouth a straight line. No sign of rage, or even a backbone. Amber looked like somebody who expected to get dumped on. Somebody who believed she deserved it.

How can I help her? I wondered, wishing Madame was there. My French teacher was probably too busy being Cal's

Placement Specialist to worry about my need for a Consultant. To reassure myself, I felt for the cell phone in my pocket. It was still there, next to Madame's business card and my wad of cash. I felt stronger, knowing I could call for backup. Or, if Homefree failed to send help, I could buy a couple bus tickets for Amber and me. But where to? And how would I convince Amber to go?

Her clean glasses carefully set aside, Amber used wet paper towels to wipe the gunk from her face and hair. I recalled my last astral-projection to Indiana, when I had stood in this very restroom wiping raw egg off my neck and listening to Terra and Jolene make fun of Amber's messed-up home life.

Now, staring at Amber's composed face, a pale mask designed to cover pain, I felt a chill of understanding. In the mirror, my wavy reflection floated right next to her solid one. We were exactly the same height and build, and our face shapes were identical. Our eyes were even the same color. I was almost Amber Reston.

chapter twenty-three

WITNESS

I stared hard into the mirror, willing Amber to notice something weird, the way Cal had when we were all in Ronni's bedroom, and Rocco landed on my neck. Maybe if I said something to her . . .

I was about to try shouting, "Hey, Amber! You're not alone!" when Sarah Armbruster entered the restroom. Sarah's eyes were red, like she'd been crying. I thought that was bizarre since Amber was the victim, yet her eyes were clear.

Sarah came alongside Amber at the sink.

"Sorry for the mess," Amber mumbled, sliding her wadded paper towels out of Sarah's way.

"No, don't move. Please," Sarah said, her voice hoarse. She turned on the tap in the sink next to Amber's and lathered up her hands. "Listen," she began, "Jolene and Terra are right outside. I need to tell you something—"

Her gaze flitted up to the mirror. Sarah, the former captain of my grade school basketball team, towered over Amber, whose head—like mine—barely reached Sarah's shoulders. My reflected face floated between Amber and Sarah. For just an instant, Sarah hesitated, her soapy hands hovering above the sink. I was almost sure she was peering into my wavy face, but then she blinked and continued.

"Amber, you need to watch out for Terra and Jolene. They're going to—"

"Still trying to clean yourself up, Reston?" Terra asked. She and Jolene sauntered into the restroom and stood behind Amber. "Jeez, you're a mess. Hey, here's an idea: We're all going to the mall tonight for free makeovers. Wanna meet us there?"

Jolene said, "In her case, I'm not sure a makeover will help."

"She might as well try," said Terra. "How about it, Reston? Meet us in the center court at five?"

"Okay," Amber said, perking up. My heart sank.

"Uh, I'm supposed to babysit my little brother tonight," Sarah began.

"Not that lame excuse again!" Terra said. "Do you know how lucky you are, Armbruster? Think about it . . ."

"Yeah. Be there or be nowhere," snarled Jolene.

I wondered what kind of hold Terra and Jolene had over Sarah, the girl I remembered as athletic, friendly, and fair. Like me, Mrs. Keppo seemed especially upset that Sarah was part of the Altos. Something must have gone wrong somewhere. I had a feeling I'd need to figure that out before I could help anybody, including myself.

Remaining wavy, I shadowed Amber for the rest of the school day. Her classes didn't seem that hard. To my surprise, I could understand almost everything in her French class even though she was one year ahead of me. Maybe Madame was right, and I did have a natural aptitude for learning languages.

One thing I now knew for sure—there were as many nasty kids in Amber's school as there were at Fowler High. Amber drew snickers and snide comments in every class. Like me, she got through her day by keeping her head down and avoiding eye contact.

Also like me, Amber chose not to take the school bus home. Why subject yourself to more animal behavior after hours? Her eyes fixed on her feet, Amber walked for miles along a series of tree-lined streets. I stayed so close to her side for so long that I half-expected her to sense my presence. But there was no sign that she did. In fact, at one point, for just a minute, I had the creepy feeling that Amber wasn't really there. Although she was still walking next to me, she seemed hollow.

The farther we went, the smaller and shabbier the houses and yards became. Finally, we crossed a double railroad track and found ourselves at the entrance to a trailer park. Shades of Amber Sands . . . only this one had no clubhouse or pool or even pavement. And if there had ever been lawns, they were long worn away. Most of the sagging trailers sprouted misshapen TV antennas tortured by time and weather. This place wasn't for old people; it was for poor people.

Amber opened the rusty door of a single-wide trailer that listed sharply to one side. The stench of old garbage practically knocked me sideways. When my eyes adjusted to the gloom inside, I was sickened by the clutter. Dirty dishes, newspapers, and soiled clothing were piled everywhere. The only clear path was narrow enough to qualify the trailer as a fire hazard. No question—where Amber lived was lots worse than our trailer in Tampa, which I had bitched about nonstop.

"I'm home, Gram," Amber said without enthusiasm. As we moved farther into the trailer, a new odor assaulted me—the stink of somebody old and sick.

A quaking voice replied, "I don't feel good, so I don't want no supper."

"Okay," Amber said. "I'll change my clothes and get myself something to eat. Then I'm going out again."

"With your friends?" The note of hope in her grandmother's voice almost broke my heart.

"Yeah, Gram. We're going to the mall. To get free makeovers."

"That's nice," her grandmother said. "Be careful of traffic."

"I will."

Without further comment, Amber slipped into her closet-sized room. It was tidy compared to the rest of the place although I couldn't see many personal touches. A few stuffed animals lay sideways on her lumpy futon, and a photo in a colorful plastic frame sat on a tray table next to assorted nail polishes and cosmetics. The picture was of Amber when she was little, holding the hand of a thin woman who looked like her. They both smiled stiffly for the camera.

Amber rummaged through drawers in a beat-up dresser until she found a clean shirt, jeans, and underwear. After freshening up, she returned to the kitchenette and made herself a peanut butter sandwich. The milk was spoiled, so she emptied the carton down the sink and poured a glass of tap water. She ate standing over the sink, staring through a grimy window framed in tattered pink curtains. As I watched, her chewing slowed until it stopped. And then, just like when she was walking home from school, Amber wasn't completely there anymore.

My wavy self turned icy cold. I knew what I was witnessing. Amber Reston was astral-projecting. Somewhere else in the world, Amber was as wavy as I was.

The "situation" lasted only a moment. Then I sensed Amber filling her body again, her life force flooding back into that empty shell. I shuddered, wondering how much time had passed wherever it was she went. Now I knew how I looked if anyone was watching closely. But wait—

Amber didn't just refill her body. She brought something back with her; I saw it materialize in her hands. Amber was clutching about a dozen music CDs, all the latest, hottest hits. It was like she had scooped them off a rack in a store. With a lurch of my stomach, I realized that was precisely what she'd done.

Amber slipped the CDs into her backpack and rezipped it. Then she rinsed her plate and called out, "Bye, Gram!" There was no reply.

That's when I remembered one of Mr. Rivera's geometry lessons: *Parallel lines share a plane but never intersect.* I was a witness to my own parallel life.

Amber headed out of her nameless trailer park and down the road to the bus stop. I was right alongside her, but she didn't know it. When the Number 16 arrived, it was about a third-full. From there it stopped often, collecting people from office parks, stores, and factories. Soon I had to give up my seat next to Amber for fear that somebody might sit on me. Although I didn't understand the physics of my invisibility, I suspected that people couldn't pass through me as if I wasn't there. To somebody making contact, I'd probably feel spongy—and that might be alarming. After a while, the bus became so crowded that I had a hard time staying out of everybody's way. A little boy about five years old barreled right into me. The collision felt like a blow from a down-filled pillow. The little boy staggered sideways and looked around as if trying to see what he'd run into. I held my breath, but he didn't tell his mother. When the mall finally appeared, I was relieved.

As far as malls go, the one in Muncie wasn't much. But I remembered it fondly from my childhood because it was my first mall, and because it had a food court where I used to hang out after school. It also had a center court with wrought-iron benches and miniature potted palms arranged under a vaulted skylight. Coming from Florida, the land of infinite sunshine and shopping malls, I now thought this place looked pathetic.

I stole a glance at Amber's watch. We were fifteen minutes early. Amber used the extra time to window shop. I used it to scan for the Altos, wondering whether they'd arrive together or separately. Terra and Jolene seemed joined at the hip. Sarah was the mystery. Would she even show up? If she didn't, I figured she'd have hell to pay, but I still had no idea why.

From the corner of my eye, I spotted the Altos; all three members were coming through the main entrance. But something didn't look right. Jolene and Terra were on either side of Sarah, pressing in against her as if they'd wedged her body between theirs. The scene was almost comical: Sarah, tall and muscular, pinned by Jolene, small and sharp-boned, and Terra, voluptuous to the point of overweight. All three wore grim expressions. What was going on?

I headed straight toward them, my powers of observation cranked to the max.

"In here," Terra directed just as I approached. The three ducked into the public restroom, which was deserted. To my astonishment, Terra and Jolene spun Sarah around and shoved her into the wall. Her skull made a cracking sound against the tile.

"I'm only gonna say this once," Terra growled, craning her neck so that she could peer up into Sarah's stricken face. "This is your last chance to get over being one of the 'good guys.' You're a freak of nature, Armbruster. That's our secret—for now. But if you don't do what you're supposed to, we're going to tell the whole school about those little dreams you have. We'll make sure everybody knows you're a whack job. You'll scare the whole school!"

"Yeah," said Jolene, who was applying most of the muscle needed to press Sarah's back against the wall. "The teachers and guidance counselors will want to lock you up. They'll give you mental tests. And send you to a shrink."

"You'll embarrass your whole family," Terra said. "And you can forget about letters of reference for college."

Jolene added, "No way Indiana U or any other school's gonna give a scholarship to a nut job. You'll be stuck here forever—the Muncie Mental Case!"

"Too bad you wrecked your knee last year," sighed Terra. "So long, basketball. Goodbye, athletic scholarships! Then you had to go and lose your mind . . ."

"I didn't lose my mind—" Sarah said.

"Shut up!" snapped Jolene, and her fast right arm punched Sarah's face. She was too small to connect with anything higher than the tall girl's chin, but the resounding blow snapped Sarah's head to one side. Tears bubbled up under her closed lids. I felt my own muscles twitch with rage.

"You dream things before they happen," Terra said. "And that ain't normal. But it can be valuable . . ."

"Yeah, like knowing a pop quiz is going to happen—and what's going to be on it," Jolene said. "Or when the hall monitor's going to get sick in the john, so we can sneak outside for a smoke."

"It only happens once in a while," Sarah groaned. "And I only told you about what was going to be on the history quiz because I didn't know if I dreamed it or it had already happened. That's how it goes sometimes . . ."

"You mean, that's how crazy you are," Terra laughed. "You need us, Armbruster. Your teammates forgot about you the day you had to give up the game."

Jolene chimed in, "Belonging to the Altos is the best deal you'll get cuz people respect us. So start playing on our team!"

"I saw you guys come in here—"

We all turned toward Amber Reston, who was standing near the door. Terra and Jolene stepped away from Sarah.

"Armbruster didn't feel so good, but she's better now," Jolene said.

"I got these for you." Amber produced the CDs that I was sure she'd stolen. "I got what you wanted."

The two Altos descended on Amber like a pair of vultures, snatching at the plastic cases.

"So where do we go for the free makeovers?" Amber said.

"Wait in the center court, like I told you," Terra said. Obediently, Amber left. Terra looked up at Sarah. "Wash your face, so you look human. Better get it right tonight, or we tell the world you're a psycho."

"I'm not a psycho!" Sarah spat the words. I was relieved to hear her anger.

"Right," said Terra. "And I didn't trip Amber in the cafeteria. The difference is nobody cares if I lie about Reston, but everybody hates a nut case."

I waited until Terra and Jolene had left, and Sarah had turned on the faucet. Then I slipped into a stall, flushed the toilet, and took several very deep breaths. When I felt strong enough, I stepped out again and saw my regular, non-wavy reflection in the mirror right next to Sarah's.

She saw it, too.

"Easter Hutton?" Sarah gasped.

I nodded and smiled.

She said, "I saw you at school today!"

chapter twenty-four
UNDERCOVER

Sarah turned away from our reflections to face the real me.

"I saw you in the mirror," she said, "when Amber was washing up."

Her eyes held questions I couldn't begin to answer.

"It's been like four years," I said. "When I moved away, I was twelve."

"Your hair—" Sarah began. She seemed at a loss for words. Then she recovered. "It's . . . interesting. So's the nose stud. You look just like I dreamed you would."

"You dreamed about me?"

"Many times."

Sarah asked if I'd heard Terra and Jolene talking. I nodded.

"Maybe I am crazy," Sarah sighed.

"Maybe we both are," I said. She looked at me questioningly. I wasn't ready to explain, so I changed the subject. "Why let them push you around like that?"

Sarah lowered her voice. "Terra and Jolene are scary. They can do almost anything to anybody and get away with it. It's like they feel no guilt, so they never look guilty. And they never get caught. "

Thinking of Mrs. Keppo's reaction to the Altos, I said, "I can't believe every teacher buys what Terra and Jolene say."

"Here's the thing: Terra and Jolene only need a few kids to back their story. They've already scared some girls so bad they'll do almost anything. Amber's one. She *steals* stuff for them. You saw those CDs. "

"It's not that Amber's scared," I said. "More like she's totally desperate for friends."

Sarah sighed. "What's the difference? The more they hate and abuse her, the harder she tries to please them. Did you see what happened in the cafeteria?"

I nodded and thought about what else I knew about Amber but couldn't possibly explain.

Sarah said, "I should have stopped the bullying, but I didn't. I hate myself for letting Terra and Jolene push me and Amber around. Tonight, they're going to try to make us both—"

"Hey, Armbruster! Did ya fall in?"

We heard Jolene's voice before she appeared. Seeing me, she stopped dead.

"Who are you?"

"Don't you recognize me?" I said. "I go to your school."

"No you don't." Jolene looked at Sarah. "Who's your little friend?"

"Watch your mouth!" I said, taking a step forward.

"Ooo, tough chick," taunted Jolene. "What'd you do, Armbruster, go get a bodyguard?"

"She didn't have to," I said. "The word is out on you and the Altos."

"It is?" Jolene seemed torn between pride and confusion. "What are you talking about?"

Fairly sure I knew what Sarah had wanted to tell me before Jolene walked in, I ventured, "There are no free makeovers."

"So?" Jolene's eyes darted from me to Sarah to me again. "Who thought there were?"

"Amber, for one. She's here to get a free makeover with her friends. Only there's no makeover—and no friends."

Jolene took a menacing step toward Sarah. "What have you been telling this chick?"

"She didn't have to tell us anything," I said quickly. "We've been watching you for quite a while."

"Who's 'we'?"

I fished in my pocket and pulled out Madame's business card, the one she'd given me when we were sitting on Mr. F's couch. I handed it to Jolene, who handed it right back.

"So you got a business card. Big deal."

"Did you see what it says?"

Jolene took it again. "'Jennifer C. Papinchak, Consultant.' So? I'm Jolene Hornenbeck, but I don't need a card that says so."

"Read the rest of it," I said, slipping my eyes toward Sarah. She mouthed the question "Jennifer?" In reply, I winked.

Jolene said, "What the hell's 'Homefree'?"

"The security firm I work for."

"Security?" Jolene made a face. "More like you sell smoothies in the food court."

"Laugh all you want, but I'm undercover." I tapped the card, my confidence blooming. "They sent me all the way from Atlanta, I'm that good. "

"You're like a sophomore," Jolene said.

"I'm part of the elite Enforcement Squad. We protect people, and we prevent crime. I hear there's some bad stuff going down tonight."

Jolene glanced uneasily at Sarah, whose face was unreadable. "What's she talking about?"

"Don't ask me," said Sarah. "She just came out of that stall."

To Jolene I said, "We got a hot tip that you and your friend out there plan to commit a couple of crimes. I was planted in here to eavesdrop."

Three middle-aged women entered the restroom, chatting noisily.

"Let's go," I said, motioning for Jolene and Sarah to follow me. They did.

In the center court, Terra and Amber were waiting on a wrought-iron bench. Terra's face clouded when she saw me. I heard her tell Amber to stay put as she rose and swaggered toward us.

"What's going on?" she asked Jolene.

"This is Jennifer. First she says she goes to our school. Then she shows me her business card and says she's from Atlanta."

"On undercover assignment," I added.

"Let's see the card," said Terra, her hand out. I laid it in her palm.

"What kind of 'consultant'?" She was unimpressed.

"Se-cu-ri-ty," Jolene said without moving her lips. "She came cuz there's a 'crime going down.'"

"Two crimes," I corrected her.

"What are you, like fifteen?" Terra gave me a quick once-over.

I wanted to claim I was nineteen, but I figured that would be pushing it, so I narrowed my eyes and said, "I'm a lot older than I look."

"Yeah, well you look fifteen." Terra flicked Madame's card in my direction, but it landed on the floor. "Come on, Armbruster, it's makeover time."

She showed me her wide back.

"Does Amber know there's no free makeover?" I was loud enough for everyone in the center court to hear. "You used that story as bait. So you could make her steal more stuff for you."

Terra and Jolene kept walking. Amber stood up to meet them.

"Amber, they were going to make *me* steal, too," Sarah announced at full volume. People peered around to see who was talking. Instead of replying, Amber turned to follow Terra and Jolene.

In a voice vibrating with urgency, Sarah called after her, "Amber, they'll never be your friends! They won't stand by you! I dreamed about it!"

The Altos, including Alto-wannabe Amber, froze. Terra looked back at Sarah, a sick grin lighting her face.

"You keep talking about those 'dreams' of yours and pretty soon everybody in Muncie's going to cross the street to avoid you. I tried to cover for your craziness, but you're too dumb to help."

"Tell people whatever you want to about me," Sarah said. "I won't shoplift, and I won't stand by with my mouth shut while you make Amber shoplift, either."

Behind her glasses Amber's eyes shone unnaturally bright. I wondered what she was thinking. Terra told her, "Ignore Armbruster. She's headed for the loony bin. And so's her little friend."

"What's this talk about shoplifting?"

A man almost as old as Mr. F had shuffled up behind us. Stooped and paunchy in the ugly tan uniform of a security guard, he was squinting through his bifocals at Terra and Jolene. "Didn't I have to ask you two to leave last week?"

"Not us," said Terra.

"It was you, all right," the guard said. "One of the clerks in the JC Penney saw you price-switching."

"She was as blind as you are—" began Jolene, but Terra elbowed her in the ribs.

"You got us confused with somebody else," Terra said. Then she nodded toward me. "You should throw that chick out. She's pretending to be Security."

"She is?" The old guard studied me. "Now why would she do that?"

Thinking fast, I read his nametag. "Take it easy, Mr. Lumpach. They sent me in as backup."

"What?" I saw him reach toward his hearing aid, like he wanted to turn it up.

"That's my business card on the floor by your foot." Since I doubted he'd be able to stand up again, I scooped it for him.

"Homefree?" he read. "Is that one of those national chains, like Pinkerton?"

"Right," I said, noticing Jolene and Terra edging toward the food court. "Where do you think *you're* going?" I called after them.

"Stop right there," Mr. Lumpach said. "I remember you two charmers. Allow me to show you the front door. Again."

Terra tried to look dignified by drawing herself up to her full height. "Come on, Reston. We'll go someplace fun."

When Amber hesitated, Jolene said, "What's the matter? Cat got your brain?"

Amber cleared her throat. To the guard she said, "The only thief in this group is her."

And she pointed straight at me.

chapter twenty-five
SECURITY

"I saw her put something in her pocket," Amber declared. She aimed her narrow index finger at me like a weapon.

"So did I," Jolene said, jumping right on board. "You'd better search her."

"Not so fast . . ." Mr. Lumpach, the elderly security guard, seemed confused. He looked from Amber to Jolene to me as if he couldn't remember which of us was the bad guy.

"I'm a fellow professional," I reminded him, indicating Mme Papinchak's business card in his hand. "You've had problems with those girls before."

"Not with me," Amber said quickly. "I'm just telling you what I saw, and I saw *her* steal something."

"What did she steal?" Mr. Lumpach asked.

I was as curious as he was since I had no clue how Amber thought she could frame me and win points with the Altos.

Amber moistened her thin lips and said, "She lifted some lady's wallet and stuffed the money in her pants."

"What?!" Automatically my right hand reached for the pocket containing Mom's cash. The money was there, all right. How would I prove it was legitimately mine? Whatever happened to "innocent until proven guilty"?

Mr. Lumpach glanced at the business card and thoughtfully rubbed his chin. "Well, Jennifer, as you know, I don't have 'cause' to search you."

"That's right, you don't," I said, hoping no one heard the relief in my voice.

"How about if there are three *eyewitnesses?*" Terra piped up. "Or maybe four." She slid her eyes toward Sarah. When Mr. Lumpach didn't answer, Terra took a menacing step toward him. "Hey, if we all saw the same thing, you have cause for a search."

"You saw nothing!" I said.

"Tell 'em, Reston," barked Terra.

"Jennifer was over there, by that potted palm," Amber began, redirecting her pointing finger. "She bumped into an old lady—on purpose, you could tell—and made her drop her purse. Then she pretended to be helpful and picked it up, but I saw her slip the cash out of the wallet!"

"We all saw it," Terra confirmed.

"That's crazy!" I said. "You're making it up!"

"No way," Jolene said. "We can describe the old lady."

"Go ahead!" I couldn't imagine how they they'd pull that off.

"She was—you know—*old*," Jolene said, appealing to Mr. Lumpach. "Like you, only a woman: gray hair, stooped over, couldn't walk or see too good."

"What was she wearing?" I demanded.

"Well, glasses, of course," Jolene said.

"Did she have a cane?" Mr. Lumpach asked. "Because if she had a cane, it might have been Mrs. Ritzman."

"No cane," Terra said quickly. "But she had on one of those old-lady housedresses, dark-colored with little flowers all over it. Right, girls?"

"Right!" Jolene and Amber said in unison.

"We all saw exactly the same thing," Terra concluded. "Didn't we, Armbruster?"

Sarah cleared her throat, and for a second I had no idea which way this was headed. Then she announced in the loudest voice I'd heard her use yet, "You're lying, Terra. As usual. This time all *three* of you are lying."

"Well, who's gonna believe *you?"* Terra said, sneering. "You hallucinate."

"Girls, please," Mr. Lumpach raised his wrinkled hands as if to stop traffic. "Let's handle things this way. If Jennifer here has nothing to hide, then I'm sure she won't mind proving you wrong. Will you, Jennifer?"

"That's you," Sarah whispered when I didn't immediately respond.

"Oh, right," I said. "But—uh—professionally speaking, it's not advisable for a security officer to surrender control of a situation."

"Just humor 'em," he grumbled. "Pull your pockets inside out, and we can all get on with our day."

My mind was racing. "The thing is, Mr. Lumpach . . . I was thinking of recommending you to the home office when they open their new branch in Muncie."

He glanced again at the card in his hand. "You mean this Pinkerton kind of deal you got?"

"That's right. But they have very high standards when it comes to crowd control . . ."

His saggy little eyes brightened. "Do they hire seniors?"

"They're always open to new talent."

"Is there a meal allowance? Do they provide uniforms?"

"Yes and yes," I lied encouragingly.

"How about dental coverage?"

"Are you gonna make her empty her pockets, or do I have to do it?" Terra demanded.

"Let's see what's in 'em," Jolene snarled.

"Not so fast." Mr. Lumpach looked at me. "How about I keep the card and call you later for an interview?"

"Sure. Anytime," I said, making a mental note to give Madame a heads-up.

He fumbled a little as he slipped the card into his breast pocket. Then he did his best to stand up straight.

"Looky here, girls," he said to Terra and Jolene. "Time for you to move along now. Let's go."

"I can't believe this!" Jolene said with all the outrage of mock innocence.

"This mall is for losers," Terra said. "Are you coming, Reston?"

Amber narrowed her eyes at me in a way that was just plain hateful. Then she shifted her glance to Sarah and announced, "I don't like losers."

With a toss of her limp hair, Amber joined Terra and Jolene. Mr. Lumpach shuffled the newly reconfigured Altos toward the main entrance.

Sarah said, "Do you need to stay—for your security work—or can we get out of here? There's another exit."

"Let's go," I said.

We didn't talk again until we were on the sidewalk outside. It was a lovely spring evening in the Midwest, the air fresh and sweet, not moist and heavy like back in Tampa. I drew a deep breath. Even here, on the edge of a parking lot, I could smell lilacs. Closing my eyes, I remembered picking them with my dad from the bush that grew by our back door on Monarch Street.

"You okay?" Sarah asked. "You look kind of sad all of a sudden."

I told her what I was thinking.

"Your dad seemed nice," Sarah said. "But he didn't work, did he?"

"No. He had a lot of problems, and my mom got tired of fighting about them."

Sarah nodded but said no more. I liked her quiet way. It was like she knew when even one word would be too much. Then I remembered my work for Homefree. Who was I here to help? Until she had called me a thief, I was sure my mission was Amber. Now I wondered if it had been Sarah all along. But did Sarah need to leave Muncie?

"Could you excuse me a minute?" I asked. "I have to make a call."

Sarah said she'd wait for me by the bus stop. I took out my new cell phone and was trying to remember Madame's number on the card I'd given Mr. Lumpach when the phone rang in my hand.

"Hello?" I said.

"Easter! Hi, it's me, Cal!"

"Cal?" The rumble of his new, deeper voice in my ear thrilled me a little. "Where are you?"

"Atlanta. I just met this really weird, old guy with a messed-up bird. The man can't see, and the bird can't hardly fly, but they both make a whole lot of noise."

"Is Mme Papinchak there?" I asked.

"No. She had a meeting somewhere, but she told me to call and check on you. You okay?"

"Yeah, but I really need to talk to Madame. Can you give me her number?"

When Cal did, I realized I already knew it by heart.

"Guess what my new job's going to be?" Cal asked. He sounded excited.

"Something to do with computers?"

"Right. I'm going to have a title printed on business cards and everything: 'Logistics Coordinator.' How's that sound?"

"Cool," I said. "And important. What does a Logistics Coordinator do?"

"I'm not sure yet, but I think I'll be keeping track of people. Where are you?"

"Outside a mall in Muncie, Indiana. Where in Atlanta are you?"

"Ma'am took me to this here diner and told me to hang out till she comes back. The food's real good, 'specially the chicken-fried steak and mashed potatoes."

I swallowed. "What's the name of the diner, Cal?"

He must have taken another big bite because I could hear him chewing. Through a mouthful of meat, he replied, "Magnolia Diner. Can't wait to get me a piece of that strawberry pie."

chapter twenty-six
OPTIONS

I couldn't begin to guess why Madame would have taken Cal to James Dean Bakeman's diner. At that moment, I didn't have the energy to speculate. I had too many other questions for the woman who used to be my French teacher.

After entering her ten-digit number, I held my breath. On the other end, the phone rang and rang. At last there was a click, followed by Madame's voice:

"You have reached the desk of Jennifer C. Papinchak, Consultant and Placement Specialist. I can't talk to you right now, so please listen closely for the available voice-mail option best-suited to your calling needs . . . To leave a message in French, press one. To leave a message in English, press two."

It would have been nice to practice my French, but English was more efficient, so I pressed two.

"To ask a simple question—or to answer a question that I've asked you—press one. To ask a complicated question—one that I may have to stop and think about, or even look up in a book or on the Internet, or call someone else to get the answer for—press two. To discuss anything related to computers, please hang up and call Cal Wacker, Homefree's new Logistics Coordinator. His number is now available on the Homefree web site. Please see our 'Who's New' page."

I pressed two.

"So you have a complicated question. Please listen closely. If you want to inquire about your new placement assignment, press one. If your question concerns either academics or on-the-job-training, press two. If you're calling about an ethical dilemma, such as an ambiguous mission or a conflict of interests, press three. If you're calling because you don't understand why something isn't turning out the way you want it to, please hang up and get over it."

I had to listen to those options twice. I wasn't sure if my confusion about Amber and Sarah qualified as "press three" or "hang up and get over it." Finally, I pressed three.

"Congratulations. You have an ethical dilemma. That may not sound like a good thing, but trust me, it is. Solving ethical dilemmas is a sign of maturity, a quality we promote at Homefree. That's why I'm going to leave the solution to your dilemma up to you."

I groaned. But Mme Papinchak's message wasn't quite over.

"The last thing you probably want to hear right now is more questions. Believe it or not, asking the right questions is the key to making the right decision, especially when you have to answer all the questions yourself. So go through the following list, and then you'll know what to do. At least that's the theory."

The recorded version of Madame cleared her throat before continuing.

"One: Are you listening, I mean really listening, to the people involved? Do you hear what they're saying about themselves and what they want?

"Two: How much of a difference can *you* make? Is this a situation where you have real influence, or are you just kidding yourself?

"Three (and this is the Big Question): Does the person you want to help actually want your help?"

Wow. Madame had pretty much summed it up.

Then she added, "Thank you for calling. *Plus ça change, plus c'est la même chose.*"

Translation: The more something changes, the more it stays the same. I had never understood that proverb. Now I was beginning to. Maybe.

Not only was Sarah waiting for me at the bus stop, as promised, but she had food. While I was busy with Madame's voicemail, Sarah had ducked back into the mall and bought us each a smoothie and a Southwestern vegetable wrap. My mouth watered at the sight.

"I didn't have time to eat, and I thought maybe you didn't either—since you're working undercover and all," Sarah said. The way she put it, I knew she wanted to know more about what I was up to, but she wasn't going to push.

Gratefully I accepted the food.

"Did you really dream about Terra and Jolene and Amber?" I said.

"Yeah. A few times. But the dreams were in pieces, like a broken puzzle. I got a real bad feeling about it."

Sarah watched me devouring my wrap.

"You must be starving," she said.

I nodded. "I think I missed a few meals."

In fact, my last one had been at the DQ in Wheeling on Saturday.

"What day of the week is it here?" I asked.

"The same day of the week it is in Atlanta."

"Right. But I came by way of West Virginia." That made no sense, so I added, "I haven't had time to look at a calendar lately."

"It's Friday," she said. "Only three more weeks of school."

"You don't look too happy about it."

Sarah stared off across the mall parking lot. "I guess. It's just that . . ."

I waited for her to continue, but she took another bite of her wrap and silently gazed into space as she chewed.

"What is it?" I said at last.

When she looked at me, there were tears in her eyes.

"My parents are getting divorced, just like yours did."

"I'm sorry to hear that," I said, meaning it.

"Thanks. My little brother's going to live with my mom, but I get to choose who I want to live with. And the truth is . . ." Sarah sighed deeply. "I don't want to live with either of them. They're too angry and messed up. My mom says I'm just being selfish, and maybe I am, but they're both selfish, too. I can't help it if they decided to tear our home apart. Maybe I don't want to spend my senior year watching them try to start all over. They don't have a clue what to do."

The anger in Sarah's voice sent a slicing pain through me. I knew exactly what she was feeling.

"Sounds like my mom," I said, and shuddered. "So what are your options?"

"Flip a coin. Heads—I go live with Dad in his crummy new apartment. Tails—I stay with Mom and Mikey in our house, which doesn't feel like home anymore."

Or there might be a third choice, I thought, and then a bus rumbled around the corner into view.

"Let's take that one," Sarah said, standing up. She looked at me. "I think we're supposed to."

I didn't ask what she meant. I figured I was about to find out.

chapter twenty-seven

ACCIDENTS

Sarah paid my bus fare without asking. I couldn't have expected the driver to break a hundred-dollar bill. Plus, seeing the money might have made Sarah wonder about Amber's accusations.

I picked a seat near the back and slid over to the window. Sarah plopped down next to me.

"Where are we going?" I asked.

"We're doing what I do when I get depressed," Sarah said. "I don't have a car, but I do have a bus pass, so sometimes I just ride around till I feel better."

When I turned toward the window, I could feel Sarah watching me. She said, "I never thanked you for saving my life."

"Huh?"

"When you used to live here, remember?"

I shook my head.

"It was weird . . ." Sarah began, staring past me. "I think I was nine or ten. I went outside to jump rope in our driveway, like I always did, but my dad had just washed the car, and the driveway was all wet and slippery. So I walked out into the road. We live on a dead-end street, you know. Not many cars go past our house. That day some older kids in the neighborhood were rehearsing their garage band, so it was noisier than usual, and I was curious about what they were doing. I guess that's why I didn't hear the car coming around the corner. All of a sudden, there you were, right beside me, yelling and pushing me out of the way. The driver slammed on his brakes, but he was going way too fast. If you hadn't shoved me—The next thing I knew, I was on the ground. And you were gone."

A very creepy sensation was climbing up my spine.

"Anyway, I didn't see you again for a while," Sarah continued. "And the next few times I did see you, there were other kids around, so I didn't want to say anything in front of them. And, well, you always acted like nothing had happened. So after a while . . . I almost wondered if it really did."

"It really did," I whispered, as so much of who I was—who I am—suddenly clicked into place.

Sarah cleared her throat. "There's something else you should know. Besides dreaming you'd come back to Muncie, looking just like you do, I dreamed you and I would be sitting on this bus together." She lowered her voice. "And that old lady in the purple dress would be sitting right over there . . ."

Before I could follow Sarah's gaze, three things happened almost simultaneously: the brakes on the bus shrieked, something crashed into us, and Sarah and I, along with the old lady in the purple dress and lots of other passengers, tumbled from our seats.

The next few minutes were chaos. I was unhurt—except for some scrapes—and Sarah was, too, but a few people weren't so lucky. Before I could pick myself up, I heard their screams, and I knew they needed help.

Sarah scrambled to her feet first.

"Does anybody here know first aid?" the driver called out. He was already heading toward the injured passengers.

"I do!" Sarah said as she moved to assist him.

"What can I do?" I said, stumbling after her. "I don't know first aid!"

"Just do what we tell you," Sarah said. "And don't panic."

I can't remember what they told me, but I know I followed directions, and I stayed calm. Mostly, I think, I held people's hands and reassured them. It wasn't long before I heard sirens coming from every direction. I was still holding the knobby hand of the woman in the purple dress, stroking the bruised paper-thin skin on her arm and telling her she'd be fine when a paramedic appeared beside me. He told me I could let go. At first I said no. That's how protective I felt toward the old lady. But the paramedic promised he'd take good care of her.

When I released her hand and stood up, I was woozy. Maybe I staggered a little because Sarah was there, telling me to sit down and breathe, which I did. She reached past me to open a window so I would have fresh air. That was when we both heard it—Amber Reston's voice in the high-pitched cry of hysteria.

"They *made* me steal the car! Of course I didn't tell them I couldn't drive. I wanted them to *like* me!"

I peered out in time to see Terra, strapped to a gurney, being loaded into an ambulance. Jolene was trying to climb in with her, but an EMT pulled her back. As the ambulance drove away, Jolene sagged against a telephone pole, sobbing and holding herself with both arms.

Amber, her glasses gone, was flanked by two officers with notepads. They all stood near a bright yellow Mustang convertible, whose front end was now meshed with the right front corner of our bus. I made my way down the aisle toward the exit.

"Where are you going?" Sarah asked, hurrying after me.

"I need to see Amber," I said.

"Why?"

"I have to help her."

"Can you do that?"

I paused. "I don't know, but I think I'm supposed to try."

As I approached, Amber was wailing about how her grandmother needed her, and now what would happen? What would happen to all of them?

"You should have thought of that before you stole the car," one officer said.

Suddenly Jolene was there, pitching herself onto Amber, claws slashing.

"If she dies, you killed her!" Jolene screamed. "You killed Terra!"

She flailed away at Amber's face and upper body with such frenzy that it took both police officers to remove and restrain her. "You're going to jail just like your mother!" Jolene yelled as they dragged her toward a squad car. "I hope you rot in there!"

Amber's hands covered her face, and she bent forward from the waist like she was going to puke. I waited a moment and then realized what was happening. Amber was trying to astral-project. Or maybe teleport. She wanted to use her special powers to escape. But they were not working.

I stepped toward her.

"Amber?" I said softly.

She moaned but didn't look at me or straighten up. Then her whole body was wracked by a gasping, gulping sob that ended with "I just wanted them to like me!"

"Amber," I repeated, my throat totally dry. "I—"

Part of me wanted to say that I understood about astral-projecting and teleporting because I did it, too.

But what came out was, "I could have been you."

When Amber looked at me, I saw no recognition in her red, swollen eyes.

"You're not like me," she said, her voice flat. "You don't know how it feels to want friends so bad that you'd do anything."

"You're right," I said. Into her palm I pressed the three folded one-hundred-dollar bills that she would have framed me for stealing.

"You'll need this," I said. "Or your grandmother will." And I walked away.

Sarah was waiting for me, a cell phone in her hand.

"I called my mom," she said. "She's coming to pick us up."

chapter twenty-eight
FINDER

When Mrs. Armbruster showed up in her blue mini-van, she wasn't alone. Sarah's four-year-old brother Mikey was with her. And so was Mme Papinchak. I almost fainted when she opened the rear passenger-side door. Mrs. Armbruster had already leaped out of the vehicle and rushed to hug Sarah, Mikey scrambling after her. Madame stayed back a respectable distance, observing the scene.

I wondered if I was the only one who could see her.

Then Mrs. Armbruster exclaimed, "Easter Hutton! How nice to have you back in Muncie." She blinked back tears of relief over her daughter's safety. "When Sarah called, your supervisor was at our house explaining the Homefree program."

"She was?" I gaped at Madame, who finally acknowledged me with a nod. Had she known all along that Sarah was "the one"? If so, why on earth didn't she tell me?

"I was explaining to Mrs. Armbruster that Homefree can provide one-of-a-kind opportunities for Sarah as she completes her high school career," Madame said.

Sarah asked, "Are you recruiting me to work security with Easter?"

"Security?" Madame and Mrs. Armbruster asked simultaneously. Then Madame arched an eyebrow at me.

"Part of my cover," I told her. "Oh—and don't be surprised if you get a call from a Mr. Lumpach. He's looking for work, and he expects free uniforms and a meal allowance."

When Madame didn't reply, Sarah looked puzzled. "Easter, are you really undercover security?"

"Not exactly. Mme Papinchak can explain everything. Eventually . . ."

"Papinchak?" repeated Sarah, perking up. "As in *Jennifer* from *Atlanta?* I thought that was your alias."

"Uh—it was," I said, not looking at Madame, who observed dryly, "You must have had an interesting day."

The police took our witness statements, which probably wouldn't help since neither Sarah nor I had seen Amber plow into the bus. Then we all got into Mrs. Armbruster's minivan and drove back to my old neighborhood. In fact, we went right past 47 Monarch Street, the little brick house with the dark green roof where I lived until I was almost twelve. It looked, I don't know, *lonely* without our family living there, kind of like an old dog who got left behind when we moved on.

Emotions flooded me, not only happy memories of my dad, but also painful recollections of my parents fighting and our family slowly falling apart. Then I thought about Terra living there, and how at that very moment she was in the hospital, possibly on the edge of death. Even though I hadn't liked a thing about her, I realized that there were people in her life who loved her, people who were desperately worried about her right now. I said a small prayer to whoever might be listening up there that she would be all right. Who knows, maybe after this experience, she'd become a better person. And even if she didn't, she still shouldn't have to die so young.

The Armbruster house hadn't changed much. Except that Mikey, who was a brand new baby in a crib when we moved away, was now walking and talking nonstop. And Mr. Armbruster was gone.

Sarah's mom was one of those old-fashioned types who tries to make everybody feel right at home. So I wasn't surprised when she said she was going to serve milk and cookies (for real), and she asked Sarah and Mikey to help her in the kitchen. That gave Madame and me some private time in the family room.

"Why is Cal waiting for you at the Magnolia Diner?" I asked.

"Actually, he's waiting for you," Madame said. She checked her watch. "And you need to leave in five minutes."

"You expect me to just zap myself there? In case you forgot, I've never traveled that way on purpose."

"You can handle it."

"You expect me to project myself from Muncie all the way to the Magnolia Diner? And just 'arrive' there, without causing a scene?"

"I didn't say you couldn't cause a scene," Madame said, smiling at last. "You already know how to get there, Easter. It's a question of focus and will."

"You mean all I have to do is focus on astral-projecting somewhere and then, if I want to get there badly enough, I will?"

"Basically," said Madame. "But let's get the terminology straight: in this case, you'll be teleporting—taking your whole body—so that Cal will know you're there."

"Cal knew I was in Ronni's room when I was wavy—I mean, astral-projecting."

Madame nodded. "Because Cal's a Sensitive. For this job, though, everyone will need to see you."

That sounded ominous. Before I could ask what the job was, Mrs. Armbruster was back with a plate of Toll House cookies. Sarah served us each a tall glass of milk, and Mikey passed out paper napkins already gooey with melted chocolate.

"You were telling me why I should consider sending Sarah to Homefree," Mrs. Armbruster said to Madame. Sarah's mother lifted an eight-by-ten glossy brochure from the coffee table and opened it. On the cover, I read:

Homefree—A Fresh Start for Your Special Teen

"According to this," Mrs. Armbruster said, "Sarah would live in another town and have a whole new life away from her family. Why would I want her to do that?"

Madame patted her lips with her napkin. "Because you love her and know that living in Muncie, Indiana, is not her destiny."

Mrs. Armbruster swallowed hard although she hadn't yet picked up a cookie. "My family has lived in Indiana for six generations."

Madame smiled. "Sarah will always be from Indiana. But she has special needs and talents. Surely you realize that a psychic dreamer can't bloom here."

"Psychic dreamer?" Sarah echoed. "Is that what I am?"

"We don't know that, dear," Mrs. Armbruster said quickly. To Madame, she said, "It's just a coincidence that her dreams sometimes come true. Even a broken clock is right twice a day."

Clearly, this was something about her daughter that Mrs. Armbruster worked very hard to deny. Madame wasn't playing along.

"This has nothing to do with broken clocks or coincidences," she said. "Your daughter has been blessed with psychic gifts, and Homefree is where she belongs. We're the only organization that recruits, educates, and nurtures adolescents with outstanding paranormal talents."

"Paranormal?" Mrs. Armbruster looked horrified.

"That doesn't mean *abnormal,"* Madame said quickly. "It means extraordinary. Your daughter's talents set her apart from the mainstream. That's why Mr. Fairless founded Homefree."

"Who's Mr. Fairless?" asked Sarah. Her mother probably wanted to ask the same question but was too distressed to speak. I couldn't wait to hear Madame's answer.

"Mr. Fairless—like Sarah, Easter, and me—was born with paranormal talents. His family—like your family—misunderstood his gifts. Feared them, actually. When Mr. Fairless' parents died, he inherited a large fortune. He founded Homefree to serve teens who reminded him of himself."

I cringed to think I could be anything like Mr. F.

"Did you say . . . *you* have . . . paranormal talents?" Mrs. Armbruster asked Madame.

My French teacher smiled. "Indeed. It's why I enjoy working for Homefree."

"As—um—" Mrs. Armbruster began, fumbling with a business card that Madame must have given her earlier. I wondered if it was the Consultant card, the Placement Specialist card, or a different card altogether. "Aptitude Analyst. So your job is to assess a teen's . . . 'talents'?"

"That's part of my job," agreed Madame. "I also work with the parents so that they understand why their teens will be better off with Homefree."

"What about Sarah's education? Will she learn math and science—or just, you know, *magic?*"

"This is not about magic," Madame said sternly. "This is about developing the talents we've been given and using them for good. Yes, Sarah will continue to study a regular high school curriculum in addition to preternatural skills."

"I see," Mrs. Armbruster said although you could tell that she didn't.

Madame continued, "We're affiliated with a top-notch private school. From there most of our students go on to the four-year university of their choice. Others continue with us to receive specialized training—in computer science or health care technology, for example. Well-paid jobs that align with their other gifts."

I thought of Cal's computer skills and wondered how Homefree would train him.

"But how do I know you'll take good care of Sarah?" Mrs. Armbruster said.

"Because we make that pledge to you," replied Madame. "It's spelled out in our brochure, on pages two through four. And it's also covered in our contract. Sarah will never stop being your daughter. We'll make sure she stays in touch with you, and of course you can visit her."

Very quietly Sarah asked, "Do I have any say in this?"

"Certainly," Madame said. "It has to be your choice. After Easter leaves, we'll go over your placement and study options."

Madame had never offered to go over mine with me.

Mrs. Armbruster said, "I'm still confused about Easter 'working undercover.' Will Sarah have to do that, too?"

"Oh, could I? Please?" Sarah asked.

"Easter plays a unique role at Homefree," Madame said.

"I've been meaning to ask you about that . . ." I mumbled.

Ignoring me, Madame went on, "Easter identifies talented teens who need a fresh start, and then she leads me to them. She's what we call a Finder."

"I am?"

Madame nodded. "And from what I've seen so far, quite a good one."

"Thanks." I suddenly felt warm all over. Not in a weird way, but in that way you feel when people are applauding you.

To the Armbrusters, Madame said, "Easter can sense the unique potential as well as the hazards in young people's lives. Hers may be the rarest gift of all."

I couldn't say another word. Apparently, no one else could, either. But everybody—including Mikey—smiled at me. For maybe the first time ever, I felt truly appreciated.

Then the cell phone in my pocket rang.

"That's the signal!" exclaimed Madame. "You need to go!"

"Should I answer it?" I reached for my phone.

"No need." Madame looked at Mrs. Armbruster. "Is your back door that way?" She pointed toward the kitchen. When Mrs. Armbruster nodded, Madame said, "Easter has to go now. See you later, Easter."

I remembered what Mr. F had said about having the etiquette to say goodbye before you teleport off the premises. So I hastily thanked Mrs. Armbruster for the cookies and told Sarah I'd see her later. Then I walked out to the back porch. I paused there a moment, inhaling the fragrance of lilacs and thinking sweet thoughts about Indiana and the life I once had here. Finally, I closed my eyes and pictured the Magnolia Diner. I gave it my total sensory attention, imagining the way it looked, smelled, sounded, and felt.

Next came a whoosh, which would have been pleasant except for the fact that it sucked the breath out of me.

Then I was standing in the Magnolia Diner waiting-to-be-seated area, under the big chandelier that Mom had used as a spotlight when she staged her show. And I was peering straight into the piggy little eyes of James Dean Bakeman.

chapter twenty-nine
TIPS

The Magnolia Diner smelled even yummier than I expected, and I instantly remembered why. This was the time of day when James Dean Bakeman ordered his kitchen staff to bake a couple Dutch apple pies. The aroma wafted through the restaurant, making customers drool. Almost no one with a sense of smell could resist ordering dessert.

But I wasn't thinking about food as I stared down the man who had almost become my second stepfather.

"What the devil are you doing here?" James Dean Bakeman hissed. His eyes darted past me. "Your mother better not walk through that door. If she does, I'm calling the police."

"You can't do that!"

"The hell I can't. I should have done it the last time y'all showed up. Now we have an agreement, and you've got to go."

"What are you talking about?"

Just then a family of four approached the cash register, the father ready to pay for their dinners. James Dean gave them his full attention, smiling like the nice guy he wasn't. I considered telling the family Mom's cautionary tale about the cook who spits in the food, and the manager who's too spineless to stop him. But I decided to save it.

"Why don't you turn around now and go back to wherever it is you crawled out from," James Dean said to me after the family had left.

"Why don't you tell me about your 'agreement' with my mom?"

James Dean Bakeman checked to make sure nobody was within earshot.

"I'm paying Nikki what she asked for, provided she stays away from here: one hundred miles, minimum. If I ever see her again, I'm getting a restraining order."

That was news to me.

"She didn't tell you that part, huh?" James Dean said, clearly enjoying my look of surprise. "Your mama's mad as a snake on a stick. She'll do anything to help herself, but she don't give a darn about anybody else. And that includes her own daughter. You don't even know where she is, do you?"

James Dean was the last person on earth I'd admit that to. I glared at him.

"Don't go looking at me like that," he said. "It's not my fault."

"What's not your fault? That you got my mom pregnant and made her move away so your wife and kids wouldn't find out?"

He shushed me. "You didn't get your mama's good looks, but you sure enough got her craziness. Now get out of here before you scare off the paying customers."

He started counting register receipts as if I wasn't there.

"If my mother's crazy, then how come you paid her off?" I demanded in the big voice I had last used in a middle school play. The buzz of conversation in the dining room died, and I felt the eyes of strangers on me. "You owed her that money, James Dean, because you made a baby with her, and then you walked away."

Somebody gasped.

I went on, faster, "My mother had to drive almost five hundred miles to get your attention. And all you worried about was making sure your wife didn't find out."

James Dean smiled nervously at his customers.

"I'm sorry, ladies and gentlemen," he announced. "This young lady is mentally ill. Please pay her no mind." To me he whispered, "Don't try pulling your mama's theatrics on me."

"I'm speaking the truth here," I told the whole dining room. "Yes, my mother made a mistake. We all make mistakes. But unlike James Dean Bakeman, she faced up to hers. And she did the only thing she could to take care of herself and me."

"Extortion!" James Dean roared. "You call that 'doing the right thing'?"

"I didn't say it was right. I said it was the only thing she could do, the way she saw it. I don't agree with her choices, but I understand them. And I respect my mother for standing up to the man who thought he could make us disappear."

Somebody applauded, loud and slow. Then somebody else joined in. Before I knew it, half the dining room was clapping for the theater of me. Mom would have been proud.

As the applause faded, James Dean reached for the wall phone. "This is your last warning," he said. "Leave now, or I'm calling 911."

"That's not necessary. And not good business, neither." Cal Wacker stood beside me. "Sir, I've learned that goodwill comes back to you a thousandfold. And so does every mean or petty thing you do."

He laid his check on the counter and fished a ten dollar bill out of his wallet. Then he removed another bill and faced his fellow diners, who were still watching the show.

"If y'all got service like I got tonight, I hope you'll tip this good, too." He waved five dollars toward a certain middle-aged waitress. "Arlene—this here's for you. Thanks, and you have yourself a nice evening."

Cal laid the ten and the five on the counter. In a low voice, he told James Dean, "I got a tip for you, too, sir. You better stand up to that cook who spits in the food. Or one day soon the Health Department's going to close you down."

With that Cal took my hand, and we walked out.

"How did you know about the spitting cook?" I demanded.

"Arlene told me," he said. "High time this place got new management."

Just then a shiny white Cadillac Catera peeled into the parking lot and screeched to a halt at an angle next to James Dean Bakeman's Sebring. The driver's door opened, and a short, plump woman with lots of sprayed-stiff blonde hair jumped out.

"Uh-oh," I said to Cal as we watched the blonde stomp toward the diner entrance. "Somebody called James Dean's wife. Looks like she's going to fire him."

Cal's cell phone rang, and he grinned at me. "Ma'am just gave me this thing, and already folks are calling." He answered, said a few words, and clicked off.

"We're going to St. Augustine," he told me. "First, we're picking up your pal Andrew."

My heart soared. I'd been so busy with my own assignments that I'd temporarily forgotten about my best friend.

Cal looked at me closely. "You did say he was gay, right? You're just pals?"

I nodded. Cal gave me a hug. I hugged him back, and we held each other a long time—so long that the security light over our heads eventually blinked on. It was sundown, the most romantic time of day. I was in the Magnolia Diner parking lot in the arms of my old boyfriend from West Virginia, who might have the potential to be some kind of hero. Or at least a good man. He was still a little goofy, but definitely handsome—and most important—honest and true. Plus, I had teleported to meet him here, all by myself, and defended my mother for the first time in my life. I couldn't even begin to think what all this might mean for my future.

When Cal held open the door of his gleaming cherry-red car, I asked what kind it was.

"'57 Plymouth Fury," he replied proudly. "Built the same year my daddy was born. In fact, my daddy once owned this car."

I admitted to Cal that, while wavy, I'd eavesdropped on him and Ronni.

"She said Short Ron helped you buy the car. But it belonged to your dad?"

"When I was little, my daddy owned it," Cal began. "That was before Short Ron had his used-car dealership—he was selling vacuum cleaners back then—but he always loved old cars. He tried to buy it, and Pop wouldn't sell. When Pop died, my aunt needed money to raise me, so she called Short Ron. By then, he was short on cash, too, having lost two businesses. But for a fee, he found my aunt a buyer. Broke my heart to see this sweet car go."

Cal caressed the steering wheel.

"How'd you get it back?" I asked.

"I got lucky. Last year I spied 'er in a parking lot downtown, a FOR SALE sign in the back window. I called the number and asked how much they wanted. It was way out of my range. Then I mentioned that Pop died while he owned that car, and the seller said come talk to him. Trouble was, I didn't have but a hundred dollars to my name."

"That's where Short Ron came in," I guessed.

Cal nodded. "I was dating Ronni, so I told Short Ron about the car. He made me an offer. If I'd come fix computers for him, he'd make the first year of payments for me. And he'd vouch for my good credit. I took the deal."

We were approaching a stop sign. Cal gently applied the brake. Then he turned to me.

"I kept my part of that bargain, and I'll keep making my car payments. I already got me a brand new deal."

"You do?"

In the greenish glow of the dashboard lights, Cal grinned. "Ma'am says I need a car for my job since I can't *astro-project* like you and her. So Homefree's gonna pay me a travel allowance. With that plus my salary, I'll do just fine."

We kissed. I didn't think about it before it happened, and I doubt Cal did, either. But we both must have felt the electricity because neither of us wanted to stop. We forgot we were blocking the intersection until the cars behind us started honking.

"That never happened when I kissed Ronni," Cal said. "But then you and her are about as different as two girls can be. *You're* going places you can't even imagine, Easter Hutton. And Ronni ain't ever leaving Wheeling."

I recalled Mr. Rivera's geometry class handout:

Perpendicular lines can be said to occur in opposition.

Maybe I really was perpendicular to Ronni McWithy. At any rate, I was with Cal Wacker, and we were both starting an adventure. I smiled at Cal. He brushed the hair out of my eyes and put the Plymouth Fury in gear.

"I reckon we'd better get ourselves to St. Augustine," he said.

chapter thirty

HOMEFREE

Cal Wacker and Andrew Seaforth were about as different as two guys the same age can be. Yet they bonded on the road to St. Augustine.

First, Cal and I drove to the warehouse where Andrew was staying. We waited a few minutes while he said goodbye to Marco, whose assignment as a Homefree guide would keep him in Atlanta, at least for a while. By then, it was after nine o'clock. Cal estimated that we had a six hour drive ahead of us.

Andrew wanted to know what we knew about Homefree. Cal and I shared what we'd learned so far, including our encounters with weird Mr. F and his squawking parrot Wudja. The three of us laughed and talked nonstop, the nighttime miles passing in a happy blur. Andrew asked Cal a lot of technical questions about computers. And we all discussed our favorite movies and music.

Somewhere south of Unadilla, Georgia, my cell phone rang. It was Mom.

"Easter? Where on earth are you?" she demanded.

When I told Mom my location, her only question was, "So you're all right?"

"I'm with Cal from Wheeling and Andrew from Atlanta. Remember them?"

"Oh, sure," she said. "They're nice boys."

I waited for her to ask what the hell I was doing on the interstate in the middle of the night, but she didn't. So I said, "Don't you want to know where we're going?'

"Is this about that Home-School thing?" Mom said.

I could feel my jaw drop. "You mean Homefree?"

"Home*free*, right. Your French teacher came to see me about it when I was in the hospital. I signed some papers," Mom said. "I was going to tell you, but then I got distracted busting out of the psych ward. I thought it sounded good, though. *If* it's something you want to try . . ."

There was a pause.

"Is it something you want to try?" The hopeful way Mom asked let me know she wanted to be done with her parental duties. Not exactly a surprise.

"Yeah, Mom, I think I'll give Homefree a try." I rolled my eyes at Cal and Andrew, who grinned.

"That's great." Mom sounded relieved. "Now I have some news of my own: I'm getting married tomorrow!"

My stomach clenched. "To Roger?"

"Who?"

"The janitor who drove us to Atlanta?"

"Of course not!" Mom was laughing. "Roger's only nineteen!"

"But . . . who else do you know that you'd want to marry?"

Suddenly I pictured James Dean Bakeman. Even if his wife had finally tossed him out, I couldn't believe Mom would marry him now.

"I met the most wonderful man," Mom cooed. "He's right here, watching TV with me. I met him at the hospital in Dalton."

"Is he sick?" I asked.

"No! I met him in the cafeteria. You know, while we were waiting for Roger's father to die. Except that he didn't die. At least he was still alive last time I checked. After I met Dennis, I never went back upstairs . . ."

"Is Dennis a janitor, too?" I thought I saw a pattern—Mom, in need, picking up hospital janitors. She'd done worse.

"No! Dennis is head of hospital security." She lowered her voice to a whisper. "He's a little older than I am but very secure, financially. He owns his own RV!"

"And he's not married?" I asked suspiciously.

"No. His wife died. He said I remind him of her. Isn't that sweet?"

I wasn't sure. The whole situation made me nervous, probably because Mom's track record with men was so bad. I wanted to believe she'd learned something or at least was due for better luck. If I had a chance at a fresh start, I hoped Mom could have one, too.

Watching Cal in the driver's seat as oncoming headlights washed over him, I knew why I liked him, both now and when I was thirteen. Sure, it was his good looks that attracted me first, but there was more. There was kindness in Cal.

"Is Dennis kind?" I asked Mom.

"Kind?" She seemed to be sampling the word, trying it on to see if it fit. "Yes. Yes, I think Dennis is kind."

"I hope so, Mom," I said and meant it. "Well . . . you have my number. I hope you'll keep calling."

"Sure." But she didn't sound sure. Mom gave me her new number, then added, "I'll be busy for a while, what with the honeymoon and all. Did I mention we're going to Vegas? Wish me luck!"

I did. After we hung up, I told Cal and Andrew about Mom getting married. Cal pointed out that she probably couldn't do worse than Short Ron and James Dean. Plus, if her new husband had an RV, they could come visit me.

"She's done what she can for you," Andrew pointed out. "Now it's your turn to build your life. Even if your mom's making another stupid mistake, you can't save her."

I just hoped she wouldn't need saving.

From there until we crossed into the Sunshine State, the three of us talked about our parents' choices and how we would do things differently when we were their age. Although we didn't mention our special abilities, I couldn't help wondering how much mine might change my life. I figured Cal and Andrew were asking themselves the same question.

Maybe it was the Florida humidity or the very late hour, but suddenly my eyelids were heavy. Andrew offered to trade places so I could stretch out on the Fury's broad backseat.

When I dozed off, I dreamed I was at Mom's wedding. Her new husband Dennis looked just like Mr. Lumpach, the security guard at the Muncie Mall. Mom couldn't understand why he kept calling me Jennifer.

Then Andrew was shaking me awake. I sat up in time to see this sign slide by:

WELCOME TO ST. AUGUSTINE
THE NATION'S OLDEST CITY

Taking his new job as Logistics Coordinator seriously, Cal began narrating our route, which he had downloaded from the Internet and memorized.

"We're taking the Bridge of Lions into what they call the Old City. That's where the Spaniards built their fort called the Castillo."

Cal pronounced it to rhyme with "last pillow."

In between Wheeling—where Mom married and divorced Short Ron—and Atlanta—where Mom met James Dean—we had lived in St. Augustine. We only stayed three months because Mom hated the sunshine and couldn't find a job she liked. Plus, she decided we needed a bigger city. One afternoon before we moved, we went to the fort. I remember standing on the old stone wall, watching horse-drawn carriages circle the historic district. I wanted to ride in one, but Mom said they weren't for us. She said, "Carriage rides are for the people fate is smiling upon."

Cal pointed to the fort as we passed it. "The Spaniards built that more than four hundred years ago." He sounded proud to know his history. "We'll turn right at the Ripley's *Believe It or Not!* Museum. I reckon that was built more recently."

"Are we almost there?" I asked.

"Yup. Homefree Headquarters is on Water Street, just a few more blocks."

"Around the corner from Ripley's *Believe It or Not!*" quipped Andrew. "Why am I not surprised?"

We laughed, a little uneasily. I think we silently shared the same worry: What were we getting ourselves into?

Even though it was three o'clock in the morning, I could see that we were passing some grand mansions on Water Street. Old-fashioned gas lights revealed fancy flower gardens with statues that looked like they belonged in art galleries. Andrew said the homes were Victorian, which meant they weren't as old as the fort, but they'd been there a very long time. At least a hundred years.

"Ma'am said they'd leave the light on for us," Cal said. "We're looking for a big, red-brick house with white shutters and a sign out front."

"A sign that says 'Homefree Headquarters'?" I asked, thinking that would be way too obvious.

"No, the name of the private school," Cal said at the exact moment we all spied the lighted sign:

FAIRLESS GROVE ACADEMY
Founded 1968

"Fairless?" I echoed. "As in Mr. F?"

"Didn't Ma'am tell you?" asked Cal, parking the Fury out front. "Mr. F grew up in this here house."

"Then why is he living in our old Atlanta apartment?"

"I reckon he goes where the job takes him," Cal said.

I was going to say that Mr. F seemed plenty old enough to retire when the oversized front door opened, and a tall blonde girl about our age stepped out onto the wraparound porch. Barefoot, she wore khaki shorts and a red T-shirt emblazoned with the name of the school. And she looked incredibly energetic for the middle of the night.

"Welcome!" she called. As we climbed the porch stairs, she addressed each of us in turn.

"Cal! Nice job narrating the route here. We'll put your PK and your computer skills to good use . . . Andrew, I know you miss Marco, but you'll see him again soon. Your post-cognition is going to be so helpful . . . Easter—great news about your mom getting re-married. Let's hope the third time's the charm. Excellent work astral-projecting!"

We stared at her. Cal said, "How do you know all that?"

"It's one of my talents," the blonde said, flipping her long ponytail over one shoulder. "I'm Kayla, by the way—Homefree Headquarters' official greeter. Glad to meet you."

She smiled extra long at me and added, "I feel like we've already met. You channeled me, back in Tampa."

"Channeled?" I asked.

"Remember when you went off on Dustin Yarvich about his ex-girlfriend and son? You were channeling my thoughts," Kayla said.

With a shudder, I recalled that day in French class when my mouth had taken on a life of its own. I accused Dustin Yarvich of things I couldn't possibly have known, and then half the school turned against me. At the time I thought I was losing my mind.

“I’m his ex,” Kayla explained. “My baby’s here, too. Homefree doesn’t usually place families, but I’m strongly clairvoyant, and they needed me. You must be a little clairvoyant yourself. Or you wouldn’t have picked up my vibes.”

“Easter’s multi-talented,” said Andrew.

“She’s right smart,” Cal confirmed.

“Whatever gifts you bring, you’ll use,” Kayla said cheerfully. Then she led us upstairs to our rooms.

On the second-floor landing we paused before a huge portrait of Mr. F with Wudja on his shoulder.

“Our founder,” Kayla said reverently. “He knows better than anyone what it’s like to be an outsider with preternatural potential.”

Before I could ask why, she looked at me sharply. “Don’t ask him about it—unless you want that bird in your face. Mr. F tells you what he wants you to know when he wants you to know it.”

Nearby stood an oversized wrought-iron bird cage. No one spoke, but Kayla must have read our thoughts. She said, “Mr. F comes by now and then, and he always brings Wudja. Best to keep your head down and your mouth shut when they’re around.”

• • •

The next morning my cell phone woke me even though it was still in the pocket of the pants I had flung over a chair. I blinked at the unfamiliar room, fragments of yellow sunlight leaking through shuttered windows to form geometric patterns on the old-fashioned floral wallpaper. When I remembered where I was, I dove for my phone, thinking it might be a call from Madame. But it was Roger Trueblood.

After inquiring about my health and apologizing for waking me up, Roger said, "I don't want to alarm you, Easter, but—uh—your mama seems to have gone missing."

"Missing?" I repeated, wide awake now.

"We were at the hospital waiting for my daddy to die—which he hasn't done yet, by the way. I happened to mention that I needed to call my fiancé Kimberly in Kissimmee and let her know what was happening. Well, your mama went ballistic—threw her purse at me and said I'd 'misrepresented' my intentions, which I swear I never did. All I promised was to help her get her money from James Dean. And you know I did that because you were there."

It seemed only fair to tell Roger about Dennis. The news of Mom's impending marriage to Dennis relieved him immensely.

"I think I've seen that guy she hooked up with," Roger said. "Supervising the hospital security guards. He's old enough to be Nikki's father, so maybe he's stable enough to settle her down."

We could only hope.

Roger was saying goodbye when another thought hit him. "Do you need anything, Easter? Anything at all?"

I sat up in the four-poster bed and surveyed my surroundings. The high-ceilinged, rectangular room was furnished with heavy old furniture, ruffled curtains, and a well-worn Oriental rug. Hardly my style. And yet I felt at home. Sitting very still, I thought I sensed the reassuring presence of somebody who had lived here before.

Who knew what the day might hold, let alone the rest of my life? I declined Roger's offer but thanked him just the same. Today I was going to take a carriage ride with my friends.

~ The End~

About the Author

Nina Wright is a former actor turned playwright and novelist. She writes the humorous Whiskey Mattimoe mystery series (Midnight Ink/Llewellyn) and other fiction. When not at her keyboard, Nina leads entertaining workshops in writing and the creative process.

For more information about Nina Wright, see her web page and blog:
www.ninawright.net
http://mrfairlessrules.blogspot.com/